NIETZSCHE

NIETZSCHE

The Unmanned Autohagiography

D. HARLAN WILSON

RAW DOG
SCREAMING
PRESS

Cover design by Matthew Revert
www.matthewrevert.com

Introduction by James Reich
www.jamesreichbooks.com

Portrtait of James Reich by Goodloe Byron
www.goodloebyron.com

"Anatomy of Friedrich Nietzsche" by Dave Kellett
www.sheldoncomics.com

Headliner No. 45 font by Kevin Christopher
www.kcfonts.com

Raw Dog Screaming Press
Bowie, MD

www.rawdogscreaming.com

PRAISE FOR D. HARLAN WILSON

"Provocative entertainment."
—*Booklist*

"A bludgeoning celluloid rush of language and ideas
served from an action-painter's bucket."
—Alan Moore

"Illuminating, elegant, and enjoyable.'
—*Extrapolation*

"Wilson writes with the crazed precision of a futuristic
war machine gone rogue."
—Lavie Tidhar

"Wonderfully demented. A thesaural explosion. Gonzo
prose for the information age."
—*Starburst Magazine*

"Wilson has found a new language festering on the dark
side of the moon."
—Mark Amerika

"Pomo cybertheory never tasted so good!"
—*American Book Review*

"Utterly original."
—Barry N. Malzberg

"A surreal, modern trip down the rabbit hole."
—*Library Journal*

"From the wild edge of science fiction. Fast, smart, funny."
—Kim Stanley Robinson

"D. Harlan Wilson writes and thinks like no one else."
—*Three Crow's Magazine*

ACKNOWLEDGMENTS

I need to thank the distinguished faculty at the Ludovico Campus of Fostoria University who examined this manuscript in various states of disarray and provided me with invaluable feedback, namely Professors John Marmaduke, Gideon Pillow, Bill Quantrill, and Nate Forrest, the latter of whom was particularly effective at helping me cultivate my ideas and mollifying my anxieties about authorship, penmanship, slavery, psychoanalysis, Nazism, and life in general. Equally instrumental were Jeb Stuart, Pierre Beauregard, and Joe Johnston; all three of these gentle scholars contributed to the reassignment of my auto-hagiographical trajectory in such a way that I produced a very different (and much better) book than I would have in the absence of their scrutiny and wisdom. Other figures of note include Henry Wirz, Cole Younger, Jim Duncan, Champ Ferguson, R.C. Kennedy, and "Bloody" Bill Andersen—I appreciate your time, attention, and friendship. I must also thank John Lawson and Jennifer Barnes of Raw Dog Screaming Press. They do so much for so many authors and artists, and I don't know where my career would be right now without them. Kudos, as always, to my personal assistants, Stan Ashenbach and Betty Lomax, who take care of all of my dirty work, including laundry, but only when I'm too sore from over-training to do it myself. Finally, to Maddie and Renee, the best daughters a rancorous, no-filter bastard like me could hope for. Remember, my darlings: *Man is something that must be overcome. What will we do to overcome Him?*

"Have I been understood? *Dionysis vs. the Crucified ...*"
—Friedrich Nietzsche, *Ecce Homo*

CONTENTS

AN INTRODUCTION
IN FIVE NIETZSCHEAN DITHYRAMBS
James Reich

EINS

You have heard of the Madman who, beneath the slaggy ceiling tiles and fluorescent mercury of the strip lights, with blazing book in hand, demanded of the Faculty Lounge: "Where is Nietzsche? I seek Nietzsche!" For Nietzsche could not be found on the Campus. Had Nietzsche become uncool? Had he been canceled? You might have read how the Faculty shrugged their shoulders and from their mealy mouths emitted ticking sounds of disapproval. One of them scoffed: "Nietzsche? We have no need of Nietzsche, anymore." There were those present, under the false and toxic lights when the Madman asked for Nietzsche, who opened their blazers to present *Nietzsche Is Dead* t-shirts, as if that was amusing, even to them. The Madman was not deterred. His zeal bloomed in his eyes like hydrogen bombs. He would deliver blows with his forearms and with no elbow patches to soften the impact. The acute reader will understand from bitter experience that the mass of Faculty were simply afraid of Nietzsche. He was invisible to the Faculty merely because they had cloaked him in their cowardice. The Madman, whose name was D. Harlan Wilson, would suffer none of this. Thus, he became what he is.

ZWEI

Nietzsche taught how to become what one is. Oscar Wilde admonished us: "Be yourself, everyone else is taken." Except that he didn't. That was Thomas Merton, approximately, who wrote in "Day of a Stranger" (1967): "In an age where there is much talk about 'being yourself' I reserve to myself the right to forget about being myself, since in any case there is very little chance of my being anyone else. Rather it seems to me that when one is too intent on 'being himself' he runs the risk of impersonating a shadow." Oscar Wilde is not always Oscar Wilde, and he himself could not be Oscar Wilde all of the time, particularly during his late years in Paris when he was Sebastian Melmoth, after his great uncle's *Melmoth the Wanderer* (1820). At his end, Friedrich Nietzsche was not himself. Indeed, after crucifying himself on the great horse of broken Will in Turin, he was quite demented, or transfigured if you prefer. Nietzsche is our greatest wanderer, the spirit of Caspar David Friedrich's most famous painting, *Der Wanderer über dem Nebelmeer* (1818), and the compulsions of Victor Frankenstein in the same year. And don't you know that Frankenstein is not always Frankenstein? That version of Frankenstein was named Henry, not Victor. And sometimes Frankenstein's *creature* is Frankenstein. To become a Nietzschean individual, one becomes something of Nietzsche. The philosopher, the genius is a creature most becoming.

DREI

Now, the Faculty of whom you have read can scarcely open their chops these days without the word "embodiment" flopping out. They should revere this work of D. Harlan

Wilson, but they will resent it, for it reminds us of the manner in which the biographer consciously or unconsciously embodies something of their subject, certainly if the subject is dead, and one of the Faculty's derided Dead White Men to boot. Resentment is, as Nietzsche correctly understood, the most potent of drives, the most pernicious of emotions, and the essence of 20th century academe and the culture it informs, like the cerulean blue of *The Devil Wears Prada,* oh ye postmodern parents of theoretical children. So yes, the Madman D. Harlan Wilson risks embodiment, but not as a stunt; not at all. The Faculty, so enraptured with resentment, might conceivably trawl through this book and complain: you promised that Nietzsche would be found here! But, Nietzsche is found wherever one becomes what one is, even if one flirts with the shadow of Nietzsche. Behold the Man. *Ecce Homo.* Nietzsche's life has been well done not only by Nietzsche himself, but also by Walter Kaufmann, Sue Prideaux—all good books, those—and by Jim Morrison, David Bowie, Roy Batty, and a host of Elvis impersonators who are what one might call "Zarathustra adjacent." Thus "all the madmen" provoke us with their Nietzsches, and Nietzsche himself with his Nietzsches.

VIER

Hang on, Madman! What is this "autohagiography" of which you speak? Does it mock the vogue for "autofiction," a term which does not need to exist? The Faculty are restless at this! They have been tricked into believing that the author is dead, but there he is, or there she is: emerging like Lady Lazarus into the writing she isn't supposed to have had any hand in! In 1931, the bodybuilder in James

Whale's *Frankenstein* cried out: "It's alive, it's alive!" You never bought that death-of-the-author schtick. You were caught in the herd, the slave morality of critical theory. The author was there all along! The last thing the Faculty expected to find! Like Bela Lugosi: *Undead, undead, undead…* Ah, lest we forget, should we doubt for a moment that Nietzsche was an *Übermensch* of autohagiography, and that it is by autohagiography that the *Übermensch* is born? As Nietzsche understood, chisel your own pedestal, because the chiselers of reputation will likely ignore you; leave a record of your madness before madness takes you. What is a biographer, really? Is the biographer anything but the sum of the introjects drawn more or less unconsciously from the subject? Ferenczi said that introjection was a process active in perfectly healthy people, as well as in neurotics and paranoid types. One becomes what one is by introjecting those aspects of others whom one would prefer to resemble and transferring these prosthetically augmented libidinal drives back into the world, as if they were always our own, and here now is a resemblance, a synchronicity, even. Only the neurotics and the paranoiacs are unconscious of this. Autohagiography is self-canonization, and thus it also sprachs Nietzsche. Therefore, do not malign the Madman D. Harlan Wilson, for he is doing what must be done.

FÜNF

Madman, you bastard, hold still! Is this not a hagiography of the autohagiographer, this D. Harlan Wilson? For whom is this an apology? You have exposed yourself. The Faculty are ashen, aghast, turning to social media for disembodied evidence, and the opiates of resentment, the eternal recurrence of the same. Don't blame me, either. It seems that the reader of autohagiography will also live and sprach an examined, autohagiographical life ... Contagion! Empathy! Compassion! Whisper it: The overthrow of resentment! Oh, to wander above the Sea of Fog in Nietzsche's shoes. That is why we read Nietzsche, and read with/in Nietzsche, as this book does. Of course, you did not come here to read about the author of this introduction. Unconsciously, you did not even come to this book to read about Nietzsche, but about yourself. It was ever thus, pretend though you might. Self-seeking! Friends of this book, eagle and serpent, here are the blistered berries of joy, *amor fati*. Here is the abyss, gazing back.

———————◆———————

MAIN
TEXT

CHAPTER 1

My trilogy of biographies on Adolf Hitler, Sigmund Freud, and Frederick Douglass appeared in May 2014, nine years prior to the release of this new volume, which my readers have been asking me to write since the trilogy's omnibus publication. "More," they whirred.

In 2021, I received this email from my father, who had just celebrated his eightieth birthday:

> Your recent posting of Steven Spielberg's *Minority Report* on Facebook led me to Wikipedia and the financial pressure they are facing. I donated $10 and then read some of your website that told me you edited a lost autobiography of Fredrick Douglass. Is this available in paperback? If so, I would like a copy. I just read Brian Kilmeade's *The President and the Freedom Fighter: Abraham Lincoln, Frederick Douglass, and Their Battle to Save America's Soul.* It was a birthday gift from Susan. What a man Douglass was. I have the hardcover and you can read it the next time you visit.

Whenever I teach *My Bondage and My Freedom*, here is the first writing exercise I assign to my students:

> Nineteenth century German philosopher Friedrich Nietzsche built a theory of the human condition on

the following premise: *All actions are motivated by the desire for power.* Think about how this premise manifests in Frederick Douglass's second autobiography, *My Bondage and My Freedom*, then choose two characters and explain how their actions are motivated by a desire for power. Be sure to cite the text and pay attention to specific details. 750-1000 words.

This is essential context for *Nietzsche: The Unmanned Autohagiography*, an exploration of the author's anxieties, enmities, pathologies, and many untold truths. Go to the next chapter please.

CHAPTER 2

I promise this biography will be more about Nietzsche than those biographies I wrote about Hitler, Freud, and Douglass. If I remember correctly, all three were about "me," viz., my idea of a particular version of "me" that no longer exists and didn't exist in the first place. But my memory isn't what is used to be, and I'm getting older faster. Time moves in slow motion when you're younger; in your 40s and 50s, it moves more like the Hare than the Tortoise. Please bear with me. Next chapter.

CHAPTER 3

Here's a bad, 1-star review of *Freud: The Penultimate Biography* on Amazon. It was written in Portuguese and I used Amazon's built-in translator to read it:

The author explicitly states in a chapter (if we can call the confusing and unconnected notes a chapter) that his book is a kind of parasite, since it claims to be a biography of Freud solely to be indicated as recommended reading whenever someone buys something related to Freud. A few lines below the author still confesses to having used the same strategy in dozens of other books, written under other pseudonyms. I don't know why Amazon doesn't remove this work from the catalog; it's a very low-level scam. (Vinivius)

Here's a bad, 1-star review of *Hitler: The Terminal Biography* on Amazon. It was written in English. Try not to get distracted by the comma splice.

Book sucks! It was supposed to be an autobiography of Hitler, it's a joke by the author for people to buy a book from him! I would like a refund of the money I paid for it! (Kretz)

There are no bad reviews of *Douglass: The Lost Autobiography* on Amazon. Is it a racial issue? Are readers afraid to say something bad about *Douglass* because Douglass was a dark-skinned black man?

CHAPTER 4

I'm bored already.

By the way, Douglass was light-skinned. His mother was a black slave (Harriet Bailey) and his father was probably a white slavemaster (rumored to be Aaron Anthony). The frenzy that overtakes me when I write means that, periodically, I spew misinformation and soar into the ether like Icarus on tequila, but my penchant for historical accuracy always brings me back down to the ragged earth.

CHAPTER 5

I didn't reread *Hitler: The Terminal Biography*, *Freud: The Penultimate Biography*, and *Douglass: The Lost Autobiography* before writing *Nietzsche: The Unmanned Autohagiography*. I'll probably just say the same things again.

I always forget what I write, almost instantaneously, even if I do long, copious research beforehand. I immerse myself completely in the content, becoming the content. That goes for fiction as much as nonfiction.

I wrote a career-spanning biocritical study on J.G. Ballard a few years ago and I can barely remember who he was or what he wrote.

Right now, on the other hand, I'm writing a book on Stanley Kubrick's "filmind" and how "the science fiction genre enabled Kubrick to become Kubrikian" (1). Hence I am presently Kubrickian—much more so than Nietzschean, but I never try too hard when I write biographies, let alone autohagiographies. The moment I'm done with the Kubrick book, I'll cease to be Kubrickian, and while I will vaguely recollect his films, I won't recall what I said about them. Like a dying spark, I'll rise from the primordial bonfire of the auteur's *mirada fuerte*—that monolithic gaze, that swallow-you-whole stare—and never look back.

CHAPTER 6

I conclude *Freud: The Penultimate Biography* by offering readers this insider tip: "The more you critique this book, the more it will critique you" (136).

We can discuss the matter of why I am so wise another time. Right now, let's see what's in the next chapter. Go to page 23.

CHAPTER 7

Let's return to the Blue Swallow Motel in Tucumcari, New Mexico. As you know, we visited the motel on many occasions in *Hitler: The Terminal Biography*, *Freud: The Penultimate Biography*, and *Douglass: The Lost Autobiography*.

At check-in, the clerk always tells me what I can expect from my room: "100% refrigerated air," "vintage lighting," "period furniture," "rotary phones," and "docile trickster figures."

The name of the clerk is Alois Villafuerte. He used to be a guest. Now he runs the motel.

"There's a lobster in the wall," he whispers to me. "Listen."

"I don't hear anything."

"It's there. Trust me. It's harmless, though. Just don't taunt it, and try not to breathe too loudly."

In my room, I eat all of the edibles in the mini-fridge and wait to feel good. This happens in about 45 minutes.

I take a shower. I don't wash my torso and extremities. I deposit shampoo and body wash on my head, then position myself under the shower nozzle and wait for the water to deliver the cleaning solutions to my hair and skin even as it washes the solutions off of me.

Refreshed, I step out of the shower. There are no towels. I stare at myself in the mirror and wait for my body to dry.

Later, I pour myself a Perrier, turn on the television, sit on the bed, open a book, and wait for the next thing to happen.

Competent readers will realize that this next thing must have to do with a seed I planted earlier in the chapter: the old lobster-in-a-wall bit. I used the bit in my first novel, *Dr. Identity*, and I've used it multiple times since then. At first, I portray the lobster as an innocuous nuisance that squeaks and scratches from within the walls, but eventually it finds a way out and angrily attacks characters.

Not once have I ever allowed a lobster to kill a victim. Even the smilingest of smiling villains escape the crustacean's unexpected, unmitigated wrath.

CHAPTER 8

Can I give up this book please? I know I just started, but I need to get free.

The first three biographies were written in a different spirit—a spirit of merriment and abandon, if not bawdiness—by a different author and a different person, who was mostly drunk and variably "happy."

Nine years later, that's not the case.

I'm quite sober and quite unhappy, *blotted* on a daily basis by the University that employs me. I out-publish every professor at the University and out-administrate every Administrator in my capacity as Chair of the Human Stain Department, but the University only recognizes good people once they resign, retire, or die.

I make an exceptional living. I'm not complaining about my income and I'm unmotivated by money. Nonetheless, I am underpaid for the amount of work that I do on behalf of the University.

I have no interest in thank-yous or pats on the back. I require nonverbal affirmation in the form of not being accused of taking advantage of the University for my hard-earned salary and being left alone to write my dumb books.

Being left alone is the greatest gift anybody can give me.

But the University wants to eat its cake, too. It wants to eat everybody's cake. Given the chance, it would eat its own stomach and find a way to turn everyone and everything into dessert.

Nietzsche experienced his own disillusionment with academic institutionalization and the University's cult of inept, bitter underperformers. If nothing else, perhaps this linkage is worth exploring in greater depth.

I will keep going, then. As always, I promise nothing. Less than nothing, I say. You know the drill. Narrative, like life, always culminates in loss.

CHAPTER 9

Fatality is a catchphrase for alterity. And the search for origins is another symptom of the fear of death.

CHAPTER 10

Nietzsche Studies has been hemorrhaging biographies since its inception.

The best creative biography on Friedrich Nietzsche is Lance Olsen's *Nietzsche's Kisses* (2006).

The best recent biography on Friedrich Nietzsche is Sue Prideaux's *I Am Dynamite! A Life of Nietzsche* (2018).

The best (and shortest) critical biography on Friedrich Nietzsche is R.J. Hollingdale's *Nietzsche: The Man and his Philosophy* (1965).

So forth.

Biographies of Friedrich Nietzsche have begun to write themselves, but that's nothing compared to, say, Lincoln Studies. Thousands of biographies canvas the ex-president's life and times. Some were written before he was born.

Why this proliferation? How many biographies do we need before we feel like we know enough about people?

The more biographies that are written, the more we misunderstand and elude the figures under scrutiny. Multiperspectivalism erodes authenticity. And subjectivity is a hungry tapeworm. If you let it, that tapeworm will dart up your throat and eat the food out of your mouth before you swallow it.

CHAPTER 11

This book is not an autohagiography any more than this avowel is not a disclaimer or a non-reliance clause.

CHAPTER 12

Growing older involves growing into the worst version of myself. Hence becoming myself entails devolution.

The University and its location in rural America preclude me from evolving into an übermensch even as my bladder turns against me and my freckles transform into age spots.

No matter how many self-help books I read and write, the ways of Administrators and redneck townies infect me like radiation sickness, breaking me down and tearing me apart from the inside out.

Please don't misinterpret my angle of repose. I remain thoroughly muscled with a body-fat index that vacillates between 8-12%. This has been the case since my metabolism caught up with me in my early thirties and I had to adjust my diet. Now, however, my muscles don't respond to my workouts like they used to, and I have to do a lot more stretching. I must also not try to lift or move too much weight. One bad deadlift could render my sciatic nerve an engine of pain and suffering that lays me out for weeks. Without a steady flow of endorphins, there's not much difference between me and a serial killer.

Unlike the Human Stain, one thing I know is myself.

CHAPTER 13

Most of my fiction derives from hippocampal dreams and cultural nightmares. I'm not unique; our oneiric impulses and initiatives always forsake free will and esteem determinism. Here's a dream I had last night:

[*Insert dream here.*]

CHAPTER 14

I forgot to put my dream in the last chapter. Hold on.

CHAPTER 15

Apologies. I'm binging *24* on Hulu.

This is the third time I've watched the show from start to finish since its release in 2001.

I love it when Jack Bauer raises his voice; Kiefer Sutherland's cigarette-weathered vocal cords enhance his delivery. When he screams at terrorists, I experience moments of unadulterated glee, regressing to an altered state of childlike wonder and oblivious disrepair.

Few life experiences provide me with these moments. They may be an illusion.

My memory is an unreliable narrator and only that narrator can remind my sensorium what I used to feel like.

Then again, what I see matters more than what is there.

As I often explain to my therapist, my garish illusions have always outshined my guerrilla realities.

CHAPTER 16

[*Insert dream here. Don't forget.*]

CHAPTER 17

I forgot about the dream again. Like the other biographies, I promised myself I would write this one as fast as I could without looking back or even going to the bathroom until I'm done.

What's the point?

Nobody remembers the old biographies, and like those formidable tomes, readers will buy this one because it purports to be about Nietzsche and there's a picture of him on the cover. People are stupider than ever these days—much stupider than a decade ago—and my writing process involves constant piddling (e.g., making coffee, making tea, making protein shakes, dusting my office, vacuuming my office, checking the paint on the walls to see if the paint has faded and the walls need to be repainted, grooming my fingernails, prank-calling Administrators, texting my ex-wife to bounce prank-call ideas off of her, doing curls, doing kip-ups, barking out rules, scrutinizing my hairline, checking the expiration dates on Carbmaster yogurt and milk, ensuring that all articles of furniture are geometrically aligned with respect to the walls and one another, cleaning my glasses, cleaning my computer screen, adjusting the height of my Scandinavian desk chair, re-alphabetizing my bookshelves, making coffee, making tea, etc., etc.).

All day long, I write a little, do something else, write a little, do something else, etc., etc. Still, I should be done with this book by the time I go to bed. I'll get around to the dream eventually. I know you can't wait to hear about it.

CHAPTER 18

I'm in Walmart shopping for cereal. With the exception of Greek yogurt, I don't eat anything out of boxes, cans, or containers—my diet mainly consists of chicken, fish, rice, and green vegetables—so I know something's wrong.

My ex-wife pulls me backwards by the string attached to my neck so that I'm bent over the wrong way. She kisses my dry lips.

"You're really overacting," I say. "This isn't some kind of watered-down Kubrickian satire."

At the end of the aisle, the lobsters consternate in their tank. The look of fear on the butcher's face belies his capability as much as his culpability.

"Ignore the lobsters," says my ex-wife.

"Who can ignore lobsters?" I admit. "They're real-world monsters. Their claws are bigger than their heads, for God's sake. Plus, they're suffering in that tank. They know they're going to be boiled alive. Monsters shouldn't know things like that. That's not fair."

In the parking lot, I force myself to mug somebody. It's difficult. My moral compass is stronger in dreams than in reality, and I must talk myself through the crime one move at a time, ensuring that I "deactivate" my victim. I keep repeating the word "deactivate." "I must deactivate you," I tell my victim. "You are being deactivated now. I am currently deactivating you, sir. This is an instance of deactivation." So on.

Manipulating the string like a puppeteer, my ex-wife walks me across the street to the afterlife, an electric-blue oasis speckled with towering Easter Island heads that look like me. I grip the string, yank it, try to break it, but it's too strong, and one of my cervical vertebrae escapes my neck.

"Anything is possible in cinema," says my ex-wife. "Special effects are God's fairy dust."

Gently her antennae wrap around my throat as she kisses me again and the scene bleeds out.

CHAPTER 19

Last month, my ex-wife asked me why I have never written a biography on a woman. "You only write about men," she lamented. "That's misogynist."

"I admit that I've been inspired by more male than female writers," I told her, "but that's just because men write more about culture than nature. Like Johnny Mnemonic, I'm a 'very technical boy'" (Gibson 1).

I didn't tell her that my readers won't let me write about women. Even female readers.

Originally, I wanted *Freud: The Penultimate Biography* to be *Woolf: The Unabridged Curriculum Vitae*, but test readings incited mass revolt, and I received death threats, one from an elderly Dutch woman who showed up at my door with a crowbar.

The whole business was silly. I always listen to my readers and do what they say. The royalties I made on *Freud* allowed me to pay off my mortgage and start a college fund for my daughters, though, so I guess it was the right decision.

Come with me to the next chapter now. Afterwards, keep doing that, and I'll keep doing this.

CHAPTER 20

I fantasize about becoming a Hasbro Transformer. I could be Optimus Prime or Megatron. Which one doesn't matter.

Morality means nothing to me.

"In attaining self-consciousness," Nietzsche deduces in *On the Genealogy of Morals* (1887), "the desire for truth will undoubtedly *destroy* morality" (144).

Ever since I saw the first *Transformers* movie in 2007, I have considered the prospect of inhabiting the body and mind of one of these mecha-kaiju. It has nothing to do with the techno-masculine sexuality that Michael Bay depicts in the aliens. It has everything to do with cutting-edge SFX.

More on this issue in due course …

CHAPTER 21

I can't stop writing, is the thing. It's always been the thing since I got good at writing. Even when I was bad at it, I couldn't stop. It's a shortcoming, a defect, an irritant. As I admit in *Douglass: The Lost Autobiography*, "I write because I'm weak."

I've been trying to be less productive for years. I can't do it.

The world says it hates underperformers. It really hates overachievers. Well-roundedness incites a special enmity, but the Stain is fundamentally lazy, inept, nonsensical, and one-dimensional.

Granted, I have always written for an imagined, unrealistic, nonexistent readership (viz., a ventriloquized yet slightly devolved version of "me," viz., people who like reading books, looking at art, and thinking about things). Daily life, however, remains a proverbial beast of burden, and the University is the Stain writ large, embodying all of the worst qualities of the human condition.

For starters, look at all of the out-of-shape Little Men in the administrative suite.

They're hedonists. They're diabetics. Their stretch marks look like maps of the cosmos while their sore-infested folds tell tall tales with no flights of fancy.

They can't stop eating too much. They need food. They fetishize carbs, dousing everything in ketchup and maple syrup and ranch dressing.

They dream about cheese, the Administrators. Colby, Gouda—all of it. Their utopia is their Excess, and they inhabit that utopia with the intensity of an electromagnetic earthfucker.

I'm 50 years old and I'm in the best shape of my life, with abs that look even better than the ones I used to possess (and that possessed me) when I smoked a pack a day and enjoyed the fat-burning benefits of nicotine. These Administrators look like old, uncooked potatoes. Likewise the Stain.

I'm not bragging. These are merely the contours of objective reality.

CHAPTER 22

Imagine a concerted act of ultraviolence, which is not real violence, but cartoon violence, over-the-top violence, exaggerated and stylized for artistic effect. *A Clockwork Orange* gets it wrong. The so-called "ultraviolence" that erupts in Burgess's novel and Kubrick's movie inhabits the realm of possibility. On your mind's screen, I want you to imagine impossible gore, then go to the next chapter.

CHAPTER 23

That was a trick. It's as impossible to imagine the impossible as it is to enter the Lacanian Real.

Fuck the Lacanian Real. But let's go there anyway.

Roomy in here. Dusty. Filthy, in fact. Abjection dominates this vastness, although I can't describe it. The Real confiscates the Word.

In 1900, there were two billion people on earth. Today, 120+ years later, there are almost nine billion people. That's four earths to turn-of-the-twentieth-century people, all of whom are dead.

We see violence everywhere now (viz., we see violence on our screens, which are everywhere now).

People have always killed people, but surely the proliferation of, say, school shootings is more than an issue of exponentially higher numbers, more than an issue of our screens showing us too much reality, too much humanity, too much redundant pathology.

Not that it matters.

Style always trumps morality. At best, every social, cultural, biological, ontological, metaphysical, and psychological mechanism subsidizes the degree to which one can stylize one's identity. That's the only difference between history and futurity.

CHAPTER 24

The science fictions that define us require endless stores of inscrutable SFX.

CHAPTER 25

The next chapter will be better than this one and the last one despite the latter's exquisite ambiguity, aphoristic line of flight, use of literary devices, and vaguely rhythmic syntax. Go read it now.

CHAPTER 26

I lied. This chapter will be worse than the last one, full of Big Words, rogue ideas, and scatological *detournements*. I promise never to foist my absurd, superfluous beliefs upon you. All beliefs are absurd and superfluous because nothing matters but the Nothingness that awaits all of us. Notwithstanding this Nothingness, however, I still have as many beliefs as you do.

Ideology is neither an excuse nor an engine for action or discourse. One doesn't need to lean on the toilet of some ideological apparatus in order to be a "good person." We know what's right and wrong; we just don't know that it's an illusion. This was one of Nietzsche's fundaments. For scholars, it's a cliché, a banality. I'm embarrassed I even mentioned it.

CHAPTER 27

I'm much more serious than I used to be. The University did it to me. Divorce did it to me. Alcoholism did it to me. Getting old did it to me.

A book like this can't be too serious.

I started out writing very silly novels, none of which were completed or published. Then I turned to very silly stories and found my very silly stride, selling one after another flash fiction for pennies.

Consider *The Kafka Effekt*, my first book, a collection of bizarro tales that I wrote in my late teens and early twenties. I was so proud and happy when it was published by Eraserhead Press. Part of me can still feel those leaves of grass, that "nature without check with original energy" (Whitman 29).

I need to climb back into my molted skin. It's where I belong. The corpse of adulthood has robbed me of my childish antics. Everything I've done since *The Kafka Effekt* has been an effort to mask and/or escape myself.

Let's return to the Blue Swallow Motel and lock ourselves in the cellar.

CHAPTER 28

This next sequence of chapters is called "Alois Villafuerte Opens the Cellar Door and Peers into the Darkness." It will involve various retellings of the same core story in an effort to demonstrate how style is way of seeing. Don't worry about all of the repetition, ok? It's an anaphoric exercise. All you need to know is that there's a cellar door in the grass. Here we go ...

Alois Villafuerte opens the cellar door and peers into the darkness.

I run up the stairs and punch him in the stomach. Alois Villafuerte doubles over.

With great force, I push on his shoulders, sharply, and Alois Villafuerte flies backwards onto the asphalt.

I close the cellar door.

CHAPTER 29

Alois Villafuerte opens the cellar door and peers into the darkness.

I run up the stairs and punch him in the stomach. Alois Villafuerte doubles over.

With great force, I push on his shoulders, sharply, and Alois Villafuerte flies backwards, freeze-framing for a moment in mid-air, then accelerating onto the asphalt.

I close the cellar door.

CHAPTER 30

Alois Villafuerte opens the cellar door and peers into the darkness.

I run up the stairs and punch him in the stomach. Alois Villafuerte doubles over.

With great force, I push on his shoulders, sharply, and Alois Villafuerte flies backwards, freeze-framing in mid-air. During the freeze-frame, an airplane passes overhead.

I close the cellar door.

CHAPTER 31

Alois Villafuerte opens the cellar door and peers into the darkness.

I run up the stairs and punch him in the stomach. Alois Villafuerte doubles over.

With great force, I push on his shoulders, sharply, and Alois Villafuerte flies backwards, freeze-framing in mid-air. During the freeze-frame, an airplane passes overhead and explodes like a firework.

I close the cellar door.

CHAPTER 32

Alois Villafuerte opens the cellar door and peers into the darkness.

I run up the stairs and punch him in the stomach. Alois Villafuerte doubles over.

With great force, I push on his shoulders, sharply, and Alois Villafuerte flies backwards, freeze-framing in mid-air. During the freeze-frame, two airplanes collide overhead and produce an atomic mushroom cloud that expands sideways across the sky in slow motion.

I close the cellar door.

CHAPTER 33

Alois Villafuerte opens the cellar door and peers into the darkness.

Like radar missiles, airplanes crash into the parking lot of the Blue Swallow Motel as if magnetically drawn there. Every crash produces an atomic mushroom cloud that molecularizes the motel, and yet the motel remains intact and unscathed, as does Alois Villafuerte, and as do I.

I run up the stairs and punch Alois Villafuerte in the stomach. He doubles over.

I retreat into the darkness without closing the cellar door.

CHAPTER 34

Through a screen darkly, I escape from the cellar and take refuge in a nearby boneyard where Alois Villafuerta awaits me with a crowbar and a Glock.

The boneyard contains as many prehistoric as posthistoric skeletons of gods, monsters, and administrators from assorted timeframes. They surround the burnt-out husk of a crashed 747 commercial airliner. An aerial view reveals a Stonehenge-like pattern, with the skeletons geometrically converging on the fallen machine.

"There are no bullets in this gun," Alois Villafuerte smiles. "Now choose."

I take the Glock by the barrel and pistol-whip him across the jaw. His head shatters like porcelain.

The ensuing dream sequence sees Alois Villafuerte's head grow back like a gecko's plucked tail. It's a ruse. His existence, I realize, was contingent upon the head that got away.

Pixel by pixel, I watch the body of Alois Villafuerte ascend into the careworn sky.

CHAPTER 35

My use of "through a screen darkly" at the beginning of chapter 34 to catapult forward the action is an instance of misdirection that riffs on "through a glass darkly."

This expression initially appeared in the biblical Book of Corinthians and was later appropriated by William Shakespeare, Emily Dickinson, Ingmar Bergman, and many other artists, often serving as a title for a range of visual, audible, and textual media.

Permutations of the expression reified its valence and popularity, among them "through a mirror darkly," "through a lens darkly," "through a scanner darkly," and most commonly, "through a screen darkly," the latter of which underscores how screen culture has recoded the flows of desire and governs technocultural subjectivity and perception. The meaning of "through a glass darkly" in the Christian bible is ambiguous, although it clearly involves gazing at the world through the filter of world-weary (as opposed to childlike) eyes, but all permutations have become clichés to the extent that the very mention of the antiquated "darkly" alone should invoke this lineage in capable readers.

My sidebar brings us back to Alois Villafuerte, whose brief, informative loop is now broken, if not entirely forgotten. Remember him in your dreams.

I won't mention Alois Villafuerte again.

CHAPTER 36

Alois Villafuerte opens the cellar door and peers into the darkness.

He paces down the stairs and emerges into a field of suns.

It's not what he expected. And Alois Villafuerte prides himself on managing his expectations. It's the only way to negotiate mankind's impotent antagonism without sinking into depression and hysteria.

The prospect of suicide enters his mind for a fleeting moment. In that moment, he understands everything, and the gravity of his mortality takes his breath away.

Seeing his favorite vintages, Alois Villafuerte begins to drink the wine. There is life and there is death and there is wine, he concludes.

CHAPTER 37

Dead authors are the only illusionists capable of writing new myths.

CHAPTER 38

The University refers to students as "clients."

At the Ludovico Campus, we have too many clients and too few faculty. Hence faculty must teach extra classes in order to properly "serve" clients.

The University refers to extra classes as "overloads."

My base teaching load is three courses per semester and six courses per year. Given our surplus of clients, I must teach twelve classes per semester and twenty-four courses per year.

I receive $2,500 for each overload that I teach.

In my role as Chair of the Human Stain Department, I receive an annual stipend of $12,000. With my base salary, I collect about $250,0000 per year from the University. I make much more than that on royalties from my biographies, but in order to accomplish all of my daily tasks (including workouts), I can only sleep three hours per night, and I can never, ever take a day off. I work every day of the year. Luckily, I hate holidays and equate productivity with existence.

The University will not let me hire more faculty.

Overloads constitute cheap labor and the University knows it. By teaching 18 extra classes per year, I save the University more than what they pay me.

I am not unique.

One of my colleagues teaches sixty-two classes per year. She makes much less than me. She still saves the University hundreds of thousands of dollars annually. These savings flow directly into the pockets of Administrators, all of whom are multimillionaires.

I'm not complaining. I can do it. I'm far from perfect, but I dare you to produce a human being with a better work ethic than mine.

Problems occur when the Administrators convene for meetings and listen to themselves talk aloud.

The Administrators spend most of their time in meetings listening to themselves talk aloud.

In these demonstrably redundant meetings, the Administrators discuss how my colleagues and I take advantage of the University by teaching too many overloads and "needlessly supplementing" our base salaries. They want their money, and they want all of their clients to be served, but they don't want faculty to teach overloads, and again, they won't let me hire any new Human Stain professors.

Every week, I receive a cease-and-desist memo that goes something like this: "Hello Dr. Wilson. It has come to our attention that you have been needlessly supplementing your base teaching salary with overloads. Everybody in the Human Stain Department has been teaching overloads. What is happening? Please take measures to keep yourself and your people at bay. Thank you" (Krane).

I have received hundreds of permutations of this same communiqué in recent years. There is no institutional memory. The Administrators forget what they do while they're doing it. Sometimes they forget before they do it, or think it. They have elevated Kafkaesque bureaucracy to a new plateau. But is it really so strange?

This is how the University works. This is how the Universe works, too.

CHAPTER 39

I have a superpower that distinguishes me from the rest of humanity. This includes dead humans, living humans, and unborn humans.

Here's the superpower: *I don't want anything more than what I already have.*

Here's an addendum to the superpower: *I could do without almost everything that I already have.*

If everybody possessed this superpower, the world would truly be an oyster to shuck and behold.

CHAPTER 40

Sometimes I listen to online voice recordings of my favorite authors from the nineteenth century. There are more recordings out there than you think.

The first known recording device, a phonautograph, was patented in 1857, but proto-phonautographs date back to the turn of the nineteenth century, and most Sound Studies scholars agree that the ur-phonautograph was invented by Nicholas Curd in 1797.

Edgar Allen Poe's voice sounds vaguely melodic and is distinguished by a thick, medium-bodied Southern drawl.

Walt Whitman's voice sounds like Sigmund Freud's voice, high-pitched and reedy.

Sigmund Freud's voice sounds like Abraham Lincoln's voice, which sounds like Herman Melville's voice.

Donny Ennui's voice sounds like a vegetable that's been stepped on.

Frederick Douglass's voice sounds full and deep and rich and colloquial and right. He never misses a syllable or a beat.

According to a study that collects "trace amounts of cellular material (Touch DNA) from books that belonged" to him, Friedrich Nietzsche's voice sounds "mild." Specifically, "Nietzsche's vocalization exemplifies a flat, smooth, typical mild sounding voice: hued pitch, honeyed tone, low versatility in timbre, silvery hyponasal flow, disembodied texture with a touch of steel in vowels, and low head-nasal resonance (lower than expected in regards of Nietzsche's robust mandibles)" (Kerr).

CHAPTER 41

Relapses are part of recovery. I relapse all the time. 99.9% of the time, I'm sober.

Yesterday I bought a tiger at Walmart.

I went there to buy a gun, but they started selling tigers, so I got one.

Tigers are less dangerous than guns and they are equally effective home-defense weapons.

Also, if I had purchased a gun, there's a chance I might kill myself the next time I get drunk. Occasionally, getting drunk makes me suicidal.

This tiger, though—if I befriend it, I don't think it will ever kill me, and when I fall off the Wagon again, which I will, it might even turn out to be good company.

I have a feeling about this tiger. It's sitting right next to me on the couch, staring at me with its green feline eyes. In the next chapter, I'm going to make it into a fictional character. Go there now.

CHAPTER 42

I had to kill the tiger, which turned out to be a leopard.

I took the corpse back to Walmart, dragged it to the Speculative Weapons aisle by the paw, and heaved it at a cashier, eyes wide with purpose and resolve.

"That's a leopard," I intoned.

Instead of a gun, I used my refund to buy a whip. I wouldn't try to strangle or hang myself with it. I'd use my belt if I wanted to do that.

I also bought some Irish Spring and a barrel of Dove Promise dark chocolates.

Each Dove is 43 calories and includes a note of encouragement (e.g., "Be YOU-nique!"). I eat one per day, and I try to abide by the dictum of every Promise.

As with wine, dark chocolate contains an antioxidant that significantly lowers the risk of heart disease, stroke, and diabetes if consumed in a responsible manner.

Since I never drink wine, chocolate gives my body the edge I need on my journey towards amorality.

CHAPTER 43

I really have to go to the bathroom now, but I promised myself I wouldn't stop writing this book until I'm finished writing it.

I still have about 10k more words to go. Maybe 20k.

On the bright side, I have found that, if I ignore my bladder for long enough, the urge to urinate dissipates. In some cases, it goes away altogether.

I have never contracted a UTI from denying my bladder the pleasure of emptiness. Our bodies, like our minds, are hedonists, determined to siphon pleasure from every pleasure-giving source.

If anything, begrudging the desires of our organs only makes them stronger.

CHAPTER 44

I have always failed to manage my expectations vis-à-vis the Human Stain.

Viz., I have always expected too much from the Stain.

Even today, banished to a rural American nightmare, stuck here like an insect on a moldy corkboard, I expect the Stain to be well-rounded, capable, driven, perceptive, open-minded, self-aware, with a camera-ready physique that reflects a reel-worthy psyche, and vice versa.

Out one window is a toxic artificial lake; out the other window is a gray cornfield; down the fastfood-gilded street is Walmart, the center of culture. All of these facilities smell like fresh manure, even in the dead of winter.

An ideal made of opposition is not an artless coming-to-oneself, but there is something to be said for twilight. Daybreak is another issue.

I am either the mad Apollo in a Dionysian equation or the happy Dionysus in an Apollonian equation.

Either way, I am the problem, not the solution.

CHAPTER 45

Unselfawareness is the reddest badge of evil.

CHAPTER 46

I decided to have a glass of wine instead of a Dove chocolate.

24 hours later, I found myself at the Jamestown Tavern feeling more human than human.

72 hours later, I awoke in a room at the Blue Swallow Motel feeling less human than human.

The room smelled like a zoo. Dead monkeys and putrid lobsters littered the bed and floor and hung from the ceiling on wires attached to their tails and claws. In the bathroom, the corpse of a baby elephant nested in a tub full of empty guns, empty liquor bottles, and enough frayed lingerie to open a boutique. The elephant had a surprised look on its face, frozen in time, and yet it looked peaceful, as if it belonged there.

I called my ex-wife.

"I got the DTs," I told her. "I can't stop shaking. I'm probably going to die. Tell the girls I'll be all right. I need some Librium. I need some benzos. I just did two shots of Listerine to take off the edge. If I do any more I'll end up at the liquor store and the cycle will repeat itself. I need to go to the hospital. Call my doctor. Call my therapist. I'm in trouble. I feel real bad. I'm seeing things. I'm hearing things. Come get me. Are you there?"

"Where are you?"

"You know where I am."

She picked me up twenty minutes later. And another cycle repeated itself.

First my doctor refused to see me, then my therapist said she couldn't prescribe anything. At the hospital, nurses reassured me that they didn't have any detox specialists on hand. I told everybody I wasn't having fun or having a party; I just didn't want my heart to stop. Everybody said they understood and encouraged me to get help. I told the nurses I was there for help. I told my therapist that I had called for help. I told my doctor's receptionist that it was an emergency.

Hours later, my ex-wife dropped me off at home and agreed to watch our daughters for the rest of the week. (Usually, we trade off every three days and nights.)

I paced around my condo until I felt better.

I couldn't sit down, and I couldn't lie down. It was hard to breathe.

The only thing that helped was to walk in silent circles, inhaling and exhaling slowly, deeply, steadily, mindfully—but not too mindfully. Thinking hurt.

72 hours later, I took an edible and some Diphenhydramine and went to bed.

12 hours later, I awoke and sunk into depression and mania for 10 days. Then I was ok. Once again, I felt human, all too human.

CHAPTER 47

Why do I know more things than other people? Why, in fact, am I so clever?

I have never reflected on questions that are not questions worth asking.

I have never misspent my strength. Of actual religious difficulties, for instance, I have no experience. I have never known what it is to feel "sinful."

In the same way, I completely lack any reliable criterion for ascertaining what entails a prick of conscience.

Everybody knows that a prick of conscience is a polestar of ill repute.

I hate to leave an action of mine in the lurch; I prefer to completely omit the negative results, the consequences, from the problem concerning the value of an action.

In the face of evil consequences, it is too easy to lose the optimal perspective from which to view an action.

A prick of conscience strikes me as a sort of "evil eye."

Something that has failed should be honored precisely because it is a failure—this is the stuff of my morality.

Can you tell the difference between my anomalous translation of Nietzsche's shtick and the rancorous exactitude of my ostinato?

CHAPTER 48

Recently, my sister conducted an ancestry background check and discovered that she and I are 8% Native American in addition to 50% Irish and 42% euromutt.

I've been waiting for something like this to happen.

The first thing I did was announce the good news to every Administrator at the Ludovico Campus. I visited each of them personally at their homes in the Dreamfield suburbs, which wind through the cornfields and hug the shores of the farmlands that pollute Lake Cocytus with infernal runoff. Standing on their doorsteps like Willy Loman, I sold them my new identity. The identity sold itself, but I wanted to rub it in. One Administrator attacked me. Like all of the University's faculty and higher-ups, most of whom are terribly out-of-shape, he was easy to deflect and flog like a woebegone prole. I delivered more unprompted floggings, none of which raised my heart rate more than a few beats. There was nothing for me to be afraid of anymore. Fostoria University's ruling whitefolk were non-introspective dunces, but none of them would retaliate against or prosecute a person of color.

For the record, I always know what my heart rate is. It's an athlete's heart rate, resting at 44 bpm at almost any given moment. When I sleep, sometimes it dips into the high 30s.

While I rallied and railed against Administrators, I made mental plans to visit other antagonists, ranging from old bosses and ex-girlfriends to all of my current students and the Human Stain writ large.

Within hours, I became quite bored, as is my way.

And by nightfall, I had forgotten myself altogether—my new ancestry, my old ancestry, my piece(s) of mind, all of it—as is my way …

CHAPTER 49

I have to go to the bathroom very, very badly now.

I always tell my students never to use the word *very* under any circumstances in their essays, not even for effect.

They use it as a crutch-word to hide their anxiety about being underdeveloped writers. If I didn't tell my students not to use it, I would find it in virtually every sentence, sometimes more than once. For instance: "In 'The Yellow Wallpaper,' Jane is a very hysterical person who faces a lot of experiences and goes very insane. Jane explains why she is going insane by using very descriptive imagery. Her husband John puts her in a room and forces her to go insane and Jane hides from his sister who is a very dear girl" (Ennui).

Of course, they still use *very*—nobody listens to me except my daughters; not my colleagues, not my friends, not my ex-wife, certainly not my students—but usually no more than once a paragraph.

It goes without saying that I can use whatever words I want at any time on any occasion. I can say anything with impunity. Velleity. Trichotillomania. Cunt. See?

Did I provide context for that last paragraph?

I can't remember, but I'm not going back to read what I wrote. "Never look back unless you are planning to go that way," Henry David Thoreau observes in "The Beavers of Yesteryear" (44). That paragraph was tangential anyway.

Context: My lexicon is comprehensive, viz., I know all the words because I've read a million books and written millions of words, all of which belong to me now, viz., I've done my penance and put in my 10,000 hours, viz., what few words you have at your disposal are mere symptoms of my forbearance.

Regardless, in the interest of my feverish modus to write without pause, I will continue to ignore the barbaric yawps of my bladder to the best of my ability. I'm an American and nothing can stop the demons of my body from defeating the better angels of my mind, but nobody can accuse me of always trying to become something that I never will be.

CHAPTER 50

It's chapter 50!

This is going to be a great chapter.

Why does everybody with Jeep Wranglers need to wave at everybody with Jeep Wranglers? I don't like it.

I've had a Jeep Wrangler Unlimited Sahara for ten years. Every three years, I lease a new one. I've never bought a car. Bought cars get old. I only want new things. Old things break down and need to be fixed.

Since my first lease, nearly every dumb sonofabitch with a Wrangler waves at me when I pass by. All men wave. Not all women wave, but most of them do.

My Wrangler is a $70,000 model with every imaginable accoutrement. I pay far too much for the lease every month, but I don't spend money on anything else beyond groceries, workout equipment, and sizable contributions to my daughters' college fund, so who gives a shit?

Granted, more people have Wranglers in rural Amerika than elsewhere. It's a sign of shitheaded prestige here in Dreamfield, Ohio. In suburban areas, it's just another mid-level gas guzzler.

Nobody who would wave at me from a Wrangler will be reading this book, so I'm just shouting into the Abyss.

Make no mistake: the Abyss always shouts back at me. We never look into one another's eyes, though. Gazing at your enemy is an invitation to a beheading.

CHAPTER 51

Did you like how I started the fiftieth chapter with a personal experience, then punctuated it with a reach-around sidebar that milks an overplayed Nietzschean proverb from *Beyond Good and Evil*? I've done that a few times now. Also note the reference to Nabokov's *Invitation to a Beheading* (1936). If you haven't picked up on this intertextuality, you should definitely stop reading this book.

You don't belong here and I don't want you here.

Keep reading.

CHAPTER 52

Grand narratives are much less than mere illusions. And with respect to the previous chapter …

To enjoy this book, you should know Nietzsche's books backwards and forwards. You should also be familiar with the history of English and American literature, dating back to Chaucer (at least) and *Beowulf* (preferably). Furthermore, you should be relatively colloquial in literary theory, Western philosophy, religion (namely Christianity, Buddhism, and Pastafarianism), science-fiction studies, existentialism, surrealism, and post-everything. Above all, you should know my oeuvre better than I do, a simple task given my terminal forgetfulness.

Without this mnemonic toolkit, all of the book's nuances will escape you, and as we know, nuances matter much more than the bare bones they inflect.

CHAPTER 53

I can't hold it any longer. I'm going to the bathroom. I'll be right back.

I'm back. I didn't go.

"Man is something that should be overcome," I told myself, overpronouncing the syllables. "What have you done to overcome him?" (Nietzsche, *Thus* 41).

I suppose I don't need to include this kind of information in *Nietzsche: The Unmanned Autohagiography*. Then again, the book is essentially a modernist effort, and modernism seethes with scatological undercurrents.

French and Irish authors, artists, and auteurs in particular loved to throw clumps of excrement at readers and
spectators from the page and screen, but this satirical met-
aphor for the human condition came to bear in all regions
and cultures (e.g., consider Kubrick's toilets).

Modernism would be a different animal sans our animal
workings, and unlike almost every living author, my
primary objective is nothing short of the preservation of
history with an eye to the inevitable death of futurity.

CHAPTER 54

What is an autohagiography? First we must understand
what a hagiography is.

A hagiography is an adulatory biography of a saint typ-
ically written for political traction or gain.

Now we must pause to understand what a saint is. (Like
all cultural institutions, religion is not as accessible to the
collective consciousness as it used to be.)

A saint is a term used by Catholics for a priest or holy
person who possesses an overabundance of priestliness
and holiness that puts the saint in closer communication
with God.

Hagiographies formed an important genre in the early
Christian church. It was a hybrid genre that, like the Book
of Revelations, pulled from other categories (e.g., biography, literary fiction, science fiction, fantasy, horror, and
even speculative subgenres such as elfpunk, Anglofuturism,
and the "cozy catastrophe").

The first formal hagiography was written in the third
century by Ventricle, a literate slave whose master, Oakenfold the Mesopotamian, wanted to depict himself as a
leader with actual superpowers in order to instill fear in

his colleagues as well as the general population. Back then, everybody who could read believed everything that they read. The superpowers that Ventricle gave Oakenfold mainly consisted of exceptional strength, speed, and eyesight—nothing egregious, but enough to make him special and vaguely fearsome.

The second formal hagiography was written a month later by another literate slave, Carbuncle, whose master, Byron Colette Gargantua IV, wanted to one-up Oakenfold the Mesopotamian. His superpowers defied the laws of physics and included intangibility, telekinesis, night vision, regeneration, telepathy, time travel, demon whispering, teleportation, and immortality. This able-bodied overkill didn't inhibit anybody's belief in him. People were shocked when he died, but Carbuncle's hagiography was so compelling and well-written, they easily deflected the specter of doubt, and to boot, Carbuncle wisely downplayed Gargantua's impossible competence.

An explosion of hagiographies ensued.

The first autohagiography was written much later, in the fifteenth century, around the time that Vlad the Impaler became a vampire named Count Dracula in medieval Romania. The life and times of the author and subject of the autohagiography, Andrei Icon, has been well-documented by other, more objectively inclined authors since his death in 1461 by "fire in the sky," an event that was initially perceived to be a product of God's impulsive Bad Mood. It was later confirmed to be the workings of a bottom-tier, nondenominational demon. Today it's widely believed that Andrei Icon did experience some kind of unique neuronic "perfect storm" that caused his head to spontaneously buzz with electricity and then combust like a fistful of dynamite.

An explosion of autohagiographies didn't ensue.

Not only did the autohagiographic subgenre fail to take off with the same gusto or efficacy as the dominant hagiographic genre, it has been mostly ignored or disavowed since its inception. Detractors lump it together with the speculative genres, especially science fiction, a twentieth-century phenomenon that has commandeered twenty-first-century onotology and reality.

This book is largely an effort to bring more awareness to the autohagiographic project, demonstrating its importance and value for future scholarship.

CHAPTER 55

Nietzsche died at the age of 55.

Sam Peckinpah died at the age of 59, and in my biography on the filmmaker, *Peckinpah: An Ultraviolent Romance*, the last chapter is the fifty-ninth.

I like implicit order of this nature, but I do not intend to conclude *Nietzsche: The Unmanned Autohagiography* on the death-note of 55. Alas, I'm only getting started.

CHAPTER 56

I guess I could end *Nietzsche: The Unmanned Autohagiography* here after all. If you thought I was bored in the fourth chapter, I'm really bored now.

CHAPTER 57

The number 56 isn't divisible by 10 or even 5. I can't end with the last chapter—my OCD precludes it. I guess I'll keep going. I'll try to be more interesting, entertaining, knowledgeable, and fun. That's what books are for.

Let's learn about Nietzsche and me.

I have a lot in common with Nietzsche. We're both white people, for instance. It's easy to be like me and Nietzsche. All you have to do is get really smart, crave adulation, exude overconfidence, enjoy stoking the fires of people's emotional and intellectual furnaces, and believe there is at least a slight possibility that you will live forever. Grow that mustache, too.

Hold on. Give me two minutes.

I went to the bathroom. I'm disappointed in myself.

Something unseemly came out of me. I recall this passage from a chapter in Olsen's *Nietzsche's Kisses* called "My Impossible Ones": "My concepts are spilling. I should like to take this opportunity to apologize in advance for what some of me are going to do" (144).

Of course, this entire book is an *apologia pro vita sua* in the vein of John Henry Newman's 1864 defense of his religious beliefs, although I am without religion, which is an infection, a disease, an insignia of human fear and weakness and desire. The history of "civilized" human bloodshed is a product of religion, of the Big Beliefs and the Dumb Ideas of Little Men.

Which reminds me: per my recent discharge, I need to drink more cranberry juice for my urinary tract. I already eat two Metamucil crackers per day for my colon, but I should also supplement the crackers with psyllium fiber in powder form.

The anvil of history always brings us back to ourselves.

CHAPTER 58

I get depressed easily. Now I'm depressed about going to the bathroom.

I'm considering having a glass of wine.

Some days I can drink responsibly; some days I can't.

No matter what, if I start drinking and history remains true to itself, within one to three months I will go on a binge that puts me in the hospital with the DTs.

Delirium tremens.

Perhaps just one glass of wine, though. This time will be different. I'm wiser and more experienced now. My limitations, my impulses, my insecurities, my anxieties, my Darkness, my triggers, my stressors—they are all transparent to me. I *know* Thyself. I've been in therapy for years. All is well and will be well.

This is how it starts. See chapter 46 for how it ends.

CHAPTER 59

I have written a lot of biographies. You know.

There's *Hitler: The Terminal Biography*, *Freud: The Penultimate Biography*, and *Douglass: The Lost Autobiography*. I mentioned my scholarship on Ballard and Peckinpah. Moreover, I have written a monograph on an insane German judge called *The Psychotic Dr. Schreber* (2019). Here's the back-cover copy:

DANIEL PAUL SCHREBER (1842-1911) came to prominence as one of history's most famous madmen in the wake of Sigmund Freud's "Psychoanalytic Notes Upon an Autobiographical Account of a Case of Paranoia." Published in 1911, Freud's case study psychoanalyzes Schreber's *Memoirs of My Nervous Illness*, a detailed account of the German Judge's psychotic breakdowns in which he battled against numerous antagonists, including everything from God and the

Devil to his own body and lexicon. Since then, Schreber's remarkable, uniquely lucid account has leaked from the psychiatric world into literary and popular culture. Many postmodern theorists have used him as a means to critique consumer-capitalism, explore the dynamics of modernity, and foretell the Nazi ascension, whereas filmmakers such as Alex Proyas have science fictionalized Schreber's experience, representing him as a product of technologized subjectivity and desire.

Why have I written books on these figures specifically? What draws me to them? What is the common denominator, the red thread that laces them together?

Nietzsche: The Unmanned Autohagiography is probably the closest I'll get to writing my own autobiography. I can't stand people that talk about themselves, and I never talk about myself in person. Even on the page, I get skittish about the subject of myself.

When I was a boy and a young man, I thought I was special. As I remark in my campus novel *Primordial: An Abstraction*, however, "most of adult life is spent discovering the mystery of how very little you matter" (62). I wrote that apothegm ten years ago and would like to revise it here. Apropos: "The first half of adult life is spent discovering the mystery of how very little you matter; the second half is spent figuring out how to die."

Adulthood has taught me that nobody is special and everybody is redundant. Hence I'm as much of a good-for-nothing *fainéant* as you are. I might be a bigger *fainéant* than you. I don't contribute anything productive to society, and except for a few people, I don't really care if anybody dies. All I do is write books, read books, grade student papers, work out, and spend time with my daughters. I do nothing else, ever, beyond sleeping and dreaming about my Golden Age past, my Death Knell future, and an alternate present that escaped me and should have been mine.

CHAPTER 60

I have something to admit. I promise it's the truth this time.

Yesterday I stole three bottles of water from Walmart. The big bottles. Primo.

I have no problem drinking tap water, but in Dreamfield, Ohio, water is siphoned into homes from Lake Cocytus. Townies still swim and boat and fish in it, but I don't. Nor do I drink it. I have no choice about showering in it. I shower twice a day, once after my morning workout, once after my afternoon workout. Luckily Irish Spring is strong-scented enough to mitigate the smell of that vast and noxious pond.

Once a month, I buy three bottles of Primo water that my daughters and I drink from a cooler. The only place to get the bottles is Walmart.

One bottle costs $20. If you return an empty bottle, you get a $14 discount. In order to get the discount, you need a ticket. In order to get a ticket, you have to go to customer service and wait in line. At the front of the line, a confused worker will ask another confused worker where the tickets are. More confused workers will be consulted and further confused, and the intercom will be used on several occasions, always in vain. Eventually a harried manager will show up and like a Magic Christian produce a ticket.

The line was long yesterday. I didn't want to wait in it and go through *Der Prozeß* à la Josef K.

I returned three empty bottles, loaded three full bottles into my cart, and wheeled them out of the store into my Jeep Wrangler Unlimited.

Driving home, I evil-eyed three Wrangler drivers who waved at me in passing, then called my ex-wife to confess. I tell her everything.

"I just stole three bottles of water from Walmart," I said.

"Why'd you do that?" she replied.

"It was easier than paying for them."

"Will I have to tell your dear daughters that you've been arrested for shoplifting?"

"I don't think so. I've done this before. I'll go back when it's less crowded and pay."

"Will you remember to do that?"

"I don't think so. Maybe? I can't remember if I remembered last time."

"How often does this happen?"

"I don't know. I tell you whenever things happen."

"You've never told me you've stolen water before."

"I think I have. Sure I have."

"You haven't."

"Maybe I haven't. Anyhow I'm just saying."

"Goodbye."

"Bye."

Have you ever noticed in the movies that nobody ever says goodbye on the phone? They just hang up when the conversation is over. Their silence is their farewell.

This is not a movie.

CHAPTER 61

This chapter should revert to another fabulous series of fictional interludes in the interest of narrative diversity and my objective to keep readers on their toes. I will foreground, say, John Vitruvian instead of Alois Villafuerte this time. John Vitruvian was a benchwarmer in the other biographies. He only appears in two chapters in *Freud: The Penultimate Biography*. I had planned to use him more frequently, but I forgot about him. I don't remember why.

I introduce John Vitruvian in chapter 22 of *Freud*. Here's the chapter:

New character.

Name: John Vitruvian.

John Vitruvian uses delicate porcelain chopsticks to eat sashimi over brown rice only until the wasabi runs out. And once the wasabi runs out, the sashimi and the rice cease to exist along with the chopsticks and the very musculature and identity of John Vitruvian himself.

Now I remember why I forgot about John Vitruvian.

CHAPTER 62

I think we're well past the midpoint of this book and I omitted an intermission. But this might actually be the midpoint: it depends on when I run out of steam and give up.

Let's do an intermission now.

Actually, let's turn the rest of *Nietzsche: The Unmanned Autohagiography* into the intermission.

We'll begin with a prompt and end with a revelation. Between these bookends, the dice will roll, the amoebas will swim, the lobsters will shriek, the guns will kill, the screens will buzz, the Administrators will administrate, the wine will flow, the toilets will flush, the machines will win, and the monkeys—only the monkeys—will ascend to an afterlife in the sky.

Then, once again: savanna and wind ...

CHAPTER 63

I mentioned that I'm writing a book on Kubrick's science fiction in chapter 5. Thereafter I name-dropped Kubrick a few times for effect.

To be honest, this book is more about the filmmaker than Nietzsche, me, Alois Villafuerte, and even John Vitruvian. Consider this passage from Jerold J. Abrams "Nietzsche's Overman as Posthuman Star Child in *2001: A Space Odyssey*":

2001 is perhaps the greatest science fiction film ever made, and certainly one of the most philosophical. In moving images—and almost no dialogue—Kubrick captures the entire evolutionary epic of Friedrich Nietzsche's magnum opus *Thus Spoke Zarathustra*. From worms to apes to humans, Nietzsche tracks the movement of life as the will-to-power—ultimately claiming that it is not yet finished. We have one final stage left, the overman, a being who will look upon humanity as humanity now looks upon the apes. It is well known that Nietzsche tells us little about what the overman will look like, except that he or she will emerge as a new kind of "child." So, naturally, many scholars have dismissed the prediction as wild speculation. But Kubrick saw in *Zarathustra* the vision of a true prophet and looked on the future of technology as the culmination of that vision. His *2001* maps the same Nietzschean pre- and post-human stages, beginning with ape-men, proceeding through humanity, and finally culminating in a new (beyond human) form, the "Star Child," a planet-sized super intelligent fetus. Almost four decades later, this remarkable image continues to overwhelm audiences as one of the most sublime visions in all of cinema. (247-48)

Abrams goes on to say that an embodiment of the Star Child may come to pass during the twenty-first century in the form of the Singularity, an event that will see the Human Stain quashed by its super-intelligent machines. I could say more about this issue, but I've already said too much, and ambiguity is the sandbox of imagination. Authors overindulge readers. Now it's your turn to go dig a hole and piss in it.

CHAPTER 64

As in chapter 61, this brief movement "should revert to another series of fictional interludes in the interest of narrative diversity and my objective to keep readers on their toes" (Wilson, *Nietzsche* 59). I will foreground, say, Andy Conklin instead of John Vitruvian and Alois Villafuerte this time.

Andy Conklin has never appeared in any of my biographies. He's a childhood friend who moved away from where I grew up when we were in the first grade. I still miss him dearly.

CHAPTER 65

The title of this chapter is "My Heaven, My Utopia."

I was in the first grade when Andy moved to Pittsburgh, Pennsylvania, after his father got a new job. I visited the Conklins every year throughout elementary school, flying solo from Grand Rapids, Michigan. I remember my mother dropping me off at the airport like I was going to a pool party or bible study. This was in the 1970s and early 1980s. Today, forty years later, she might be arrested.

Mnemonic vestiges of my stays with Andy include backyard trampolines, bloody-faced professional wrestlers, wave pools, Masters-of-the-Universe action figures, and a department store named Higbees that Andy liked to pronounce as "*Hick*-bees." Those seemingly harmless, disposable *mise en scenès* are my heaven, my utopia.

CHAPTER 66

Sorry about that last chapter. I was supposed to turn Andy into a character.

I'm going to pretend I'm Andy Conklin now. Please pretend that I'm him, too.

You may need to suspend your disbelief in other ways.

We'll see.

I'll do this for five chapters.

CHAPTER 67

A few days ago, I went to a local restaurant for breakfast. All restaurants in Dreamfield are either fast-food chains or poorly run shitholes. This one's a shithole with an open kitchen enclosed by a bar. Good cheat food. I eat a strict Mediterranean diet, but once a week I pig out.

I sat at the bar and ordered orange juice, a coffee, and a sparkling water from a waitress who forced herself to be nice to me. I didn't say anything to upset her; I pretended that I was a happy, salt-of-the-earth-type person. Somehow, though, my mild-mannered exterior betrays my general demeanor and I rub townies the wrong way.

There were six stools at the bar. All of them were empty when I came in.

I selected the last stool at the far end.

Moments after my drinks arrived, a man entered and sat on the stool next to me.

Horrified, I stood definitely, scanned the restaurant for a nearby table, and collected my drinks.

"What are you doing?" said the man.

"I'm moving, fucker. What the fuck are you doing, ass-hole? Why the fuck did you sit right next to me, shithead? Fuck you, you crazy motherfucker. There's, like, a global fucking pandemic going on right now. Fuck me. There's four more fucking seats you could have sat down in. Who the fuck are you? Fuck you, dummy. Seriously."

During the rant, the waitress looked at me as if I had burned down her church, and the man oscillated between remorse and anger. At first, he said he would move. Then he resolved to stay, citing me for being impolite. Then he apologized and said he would move again. Then he said, "No, I'm not moving. I'm staying. I'm staying right here, you son of a bitch." He went back and forth like this a few more times. Ignoring him, I carried my orange juice and coffee to a table. But my breakfast had been ruined before it had been served. I hadn't even ordered my breakfast.

"You know what?" I announced to the restaurant. "It's my fault. I made a mistake. I shouldn't have come in here. The king's to blame, like. Excuse me."

I left.

The waitress chased me outside. "You gonna pay for those beverages, sir? You gotta pay!"

"I took one sip of coffee! I owe you two cents!"

She kept coming, so I broke into a run, sprung into my Wrangler, and sped away.

In the rearview mirror, I saw her scribble down my license plate number on her order pad. The police have not yet contacted me or showed up at my door.

CHAPTER 68

Apologies. The "I" in the last chapter was supposed to be Andy Conklin. It still could be. I had planned to write the chapter in the third person, foregrounding my old friend's name. I'll get it right in the next chapter. I should probably create a fictional setting as well. Dreamfield is more real than reality itself.

CHAPTER 69

Repeat chapter 67, foregrounding "Andy Conklin" instead of "I" in the third instead of the first person. Also include various science-fictional motifs (e.g., futuristic kitchen equipment, an android waiter, possibly an alien disguised as a businessman à la *They Live*) and change "Dreamfield" to "Bliptown."

CHAPTER 70

In *They Live*, humans can only see the aliens that have sub-liminally overtaken the world by wearing sunglasses called Hoffman lenses. I'm reticent to do likewise in the Andy Conklin bit.

Consciously and unconsciously, all artists and authors borrow from their predecessors, and the best ideas are borrowed and innovated. I always try to eschew the former in favor of the latter, but I'm the same cultural monster as you. We can't escape our Frankensteinian construction;

these refurbished body parts belong to me whether I like them or want them or not.

I said I would do this bit for five chapters, but it's not working. So much isn't working at this point. I really should end the book now.

Let me text my ex-wife and see what I should do.

Let me pour myself a glass of wine and see what happens.

CHAPTER 71

Thank you in advance for reading this chapter. As it turns out, *Nietzsche: The Unmanned Autohagiography* is a parody of the multi-tonal voice-over that plagues the screens of *Hitler: The Terminal Biography, Freud: The Penultimate Biography*, and *Douglass: The Lost Autobiography*. Collectively published as an omnibus called the Biographizer trilogy (a.k.a. the Angry Off-White Author series or Hawgstrüffel's Hot Filibuster), these nonfictional infotainments themselves parody other auteur's voice-overs, voice-overs in general, and the biographical impetus writ large.

There is no excuse for voice-overs—only Kubrick gets away with it. Otherwise, voice-overs always constitute lazy storytelling, sacrificing the Show for the Tell.

Biographies are not the "nonfictional" exploits that they purport to be. They are more fictional than most novels. How could there be so many biographies of Tom Cruise? Which biography of Tom Cruise is the "correct" one, viz., which one manifests the Truth?

There is no Truth, no reality, no objectivity. There is only subjectivity.

There are only algorithms. Hence this thesis from a review of *Freud* that appeared in *The Rumpus*: "*Ceci n'est pas une livre* ... This is not a book. It is an algorithm."

The review was written by "James Reich," a fictional author and one of my many pseudonyms. I have published numerous books under this pseudonym and hundreds of essays, articles, reviews, and other writings, including the introduction to *Nietzsche: The Unmanned Autohagiography*. Primarily, I employ Mr. Reich to write positive reviews of my work. This isn't the Truth, per se, but I'm in no position to forsake my artistic integrity.

CHAPTER 72

Thanks for reading this chapter as well. You're a very good reader and a decent person.

I was bullied as a child, mostly in the sixth and seventh grades. I was awkward, uncoordinated, afraid, weak, sensitive, goofy, peculiar—a bully's Nice Dream.

In the ninth grade, I got big, achieving a height of 6'5". I got coordinated and confident, too.

Calmly, I hunted down the dirty motherfuckers who had fucked me up, knocking them down, as Jack Torrance might say, "one buh one" (*The Shining*).

There were five bullies, all of which I left unconscious in their back yards after lying in wait for them like a wily jaguar. Thus did I ambuscade and beat the shit out of them, drawing blood every time—my thesis was to draw blood and paint the green grass red. It's the best thing I've ever done in my life. I was fifteen years old. I'm fifty now, and I continue to beam with pride.

CHAPTER 73

I was kidding about you being "a very good reader and a decent person" in the last chapter (Wilson, *Nietzsche* 67).

You know what you are. I'm just playing nice and wearing my mask. This relationship of ours, this thing we got—it works because of me, remember. The Human Stain can't adapt to anything. We're only getting along because of my ability to acclimatize to your disability.

CHAPTER 74

Most of life amounts to a war with your body.

Hangovers and headaches, infections and sicknesses and viruses, paper cuts and acne and dry skin and sprained ankles and dysfunctional organs and pinched nerves and broken bones—your body is not your friend.

It's against you.

It's an antagonist.

You are the protagonist. But there is no you without your body.

Forget philosophy: your mind is not "free."

Forget science fiction: you can't download yourself into another receptacle.

You're stuck with the flesh, bone, and gore that defines the contours of your physical self.

Which you must coddle.

Which you must make into a friend.

Or, better perhaps, which you must keep close, like the enemy it is.

CHAPTER 75

We are supposed to respect our elders, but our elders are Morlocks—not Übermenschen, but *untermenschen.* Infancy is a worthier cause. Wrinkles and wisdom are both full of lard. Praise the Hollow Boys and the pink flesh.

CHAPTER 76

Everybody steals Nietzsche's aphorisms. Watch this:

"To throw thunder, let alone breathe thunder, one must first learn to eat thunder."

That was actually my aphorism. Watch this, though:

"What doesn't kill me makes me stronger."

Everybody knows that one, which was first printed in *Twilight of the Idols* (1889). Hitler loved that one. He stole all of Nietzsche's maxims, inhaling and exhaling them as if they might be thunder.

Nietzsche would have been horrified by how Hitler et al. perverted his ideas, revising and/or decontextualizing them to suit Nazi ideals, ideology, etc. But Nazis weren't the only plagiarists.

How many times have texts told you that you'll be made stronger by something that doesn't kill you? Heath Ledger's Joker replaces *stronger* with *stranger* in *The Dark Knight* (2008), but the message (viz., the medium, viz., the *massage*) is the same.

Ewige Wiederkunft. Eternal recurrence.

Or, as Nietzsche says in *The Gay Science*: "The eternal hourglass of existence is turned upside down again and again, and you with it, you speck of dust!" (273).

CHAPTER 77

I used to write aphorisms for a magazine column. I called them "mad maxims." Every week, I'd come up with something new. I forgot the name of the magazine, but here's one of them:

"Reality is shaped by the forces that destroy it."

Wait, that's from *The Kyoto Man*.

The Kyoto Man is the third installment in my so-called Scikungfi trilogy after *Codename Prague* (2009) and my first published novel *Dr. Identity* (2007). That maxim also appears in chapter 55 of *Douglass: The Lost Autobiography* where I randomly cite the back-cover copy for *The Kyoto Man*.

As with Nietzsche, "mad maxims" infest my books like viral pirates, but the one about reality seems to be the most popular. It's even cited in the video game *No Man's Sky* (2016). But it's all over the internet. Google it. One place it'll take you is Quotemaster.org. Enter REALITY into the search bar and you'll find my maxim among hundreds of others on the subject. The one that precedes mine is by Max Beerbohm and reads:

"All fantasy should have a solid base in reality."

The one that follows mine is by Faye McCray and reads:

"Dreams are fragile. Reality is a clumsy postman."

McCray's is pretty good. Between you and me, I think mine is the best of the three. I say this without ego, desire, or even the slightest inkling or eruption of subjectivity. To reiterate my stance at the end of chapter 21: "These are merely the contours of objective reality" (Wilson, *Nietzsche* 32).

CHAPTER 78

I can't find those mad maxims. I wrote them for a print magazine. I recollect an online component as well. They're not on my computer, and there's not a trace of them online, goddamn it.

I experiment with composing aphorisms via a parodic Twitter account that belongs to a nonexistent mountebank, Donovan Ogg, the name of the virulent filmmaker and antagonist in my novel *Outré*. The account has been around for a few years and I mostly use it to collate daily news. On average, Ogg tweets about once a week. Here are some recent contributions:

"The future always spoils history."

"I am who I want to be who is not who I want to be."

"Snowflakes are the frozen tears of God's sky-bastards."

"Mushrooms shrink under duress."

"Mortality is a catchphrase for alterity."

"Americans will be the end of America."

None of these maxims are particularly good (or "mad"). Writing them provides me with a brief moment of satisfaction, if not jouissance.

Donovan Ogg has seven followers. One is the co-editor of the publisher of *Nietzsche: The Unmanned Autohagiography*, *Douglass: The Lost Autobiography*, *Freud: The Penultimate Biography*, and *Hitler: The Terminal Biography*. He goes by the handle @bizarroguy. Check him out; he's a good man and a fine writer.

I don't know what would possess Donovan Ogg's six other followers to follow him, especially @1220CarWash, who, as the username indicates, is a car wash. They are likely either bots, camgirls, or inactive trolls, three of the most popular modes of twenty-first century existence.

CHAPTER 79

Collections of aphorisms (a.k.a. "wisdom literature") were as popular as latex novels (a.k.a. "endocrine fiction") in the nineteenth century. Nietzsche despised anything popular. Like the Force in Luke, however, the aphoristic impulse was strong in him.

He couldn't resist the impulse.

His publisher reminded him that the market was oversaturated, that he would fall victim to the hot bloodlust of bobble-headed reviewers who would attack him no matter how aphoristically capable and versatile he proved to be, but Nietzsche ignored his publisher, and he made the form his own.

It's not that hard to write an aphorism. Writing mediocre or bad aphorisms is downright easy (see chapters 78 and 80). Most literature is really mediocre or really bad. Always has been; always will be. As Nietzsche reminds us in the posthumously published *Haarige Götter der Arkaden* a.k.a. *Hairy Gods of the Arcades* (1951), "I write so that I can read something worthy of refraction" (666).

I'm pretty drunk at this point. I don't think I'll make it much longer.

CHAPTER 80

I'm starting to sober up. Something changed in the last ten seconds as I shook the sleep-prickles out of my left hand. This hand usually only falls asleep in the early morning, but sometimes it happens when I write too fast for too long. Growing old is a Kurtzian horror. To grow old is to grow mold. But Sir Davos Seaworth says it best in "Eastwatch" (2017), the fifth episode of the seventh season of *Game of Thrones*: "Nothing fucks you harder than time."

In this moment of sobriety, I see a ray of mnemonic light change direction when it enters the angle of my identity. It won't last. We must squeeze the blood from the stone of this moment until the next one demolishes its essence.

CHAPTER 81

I usually deliver lectures in German, no matter what the subject is, but not with Nietzsche, who (be)gets my

American tongue. Following Anthony Soprano Jr., I always pronounce "Nietzsche" as "Nitch" when I deliver lectures on his philosophy ("D-Girl"). At first, my listeners observe me like an orangutan in a zoo, but they can't deny the prowess of the dialectic of my enlightenment. The best they can do is wince when I say "Nitch" as I feign ignorance of the correct pronunciation (viz., "Nee-chuh"). Without exception, however, by the time my lectures come to an end, all of my audiences think "Nitch" is the ur-phonation.

CHAPTER 82

Post-divorce, men may be allotted anywhere from six to twelve months to drink away their angst and drink their way back to something like normalcy, functionality, etc. Some men stay drunk forever. After more than a year of carrying on, they should neither be excused from bad behavior nor given sympathy. There's no excuse for not taking a cold shower and getting your shit together after a goddamn year of feeling sorry for yourself.

Here's a post I made on Facebook in 2015 during the second precarious month: "Today I ain't doing SHIIIIIIT ... again. Actually I'll do some shit today. That's what shit-doers do."

With no exceptions beyond posting occasional pictures of my daughters for extended family members, I only use social networks to promote my books and publishers. That's how upset I was after my divorce.

CHAPTER 83

Let's do some more fiction now.

Actually, let's do some anti-fiction.

Or some *outré*-fiction.

Or some superzero-fiction, some scikung-fiction, some *Schreberfiktion* distinguished by Hörnblowér prose.

Ennui can turn stars into black holes.

CHAPTER 84

I love my Unfamily. That's what I call it.

My daughters and my ex-wife—my Unfamily. Like the Mad Hatter's Unbirthday.

It's an Undoing of the conventional nuclear family that works better than most marriages. I've never met a married couple with children who's collectively "happier" than all of us. And my daughters are genuinely happy despite the social, cultural, ideological, and geographical horror of Dreamfield, Ohio.

My ex-wife lives down the street. We trade the girls every three days and nights. We're divorced because she's too messy and I'm too clean and she can't forgive me for the neglect she suffered during our marriage when alcoholism and narcissism were my guiding lights.

Living at my ex-wife's house is a pastoral, rustic affair whereas living at my lakeside condo is like inhabiting a perpetually self-cleaning hotel. My girls have the best of both worlds in a world of shit that they don't see because they've never lived anywhere else and there's no discernible point of comparison.

CHAPTER 85

On the next two pages, please find my favorite chapter from *Douglass: The Lost Autobiography*. It's chapter 42, a number that bears no significance whatsoever.

CHAPTER 42

Somebody set a monkey loose at the Blue Swallow Motel.

"Kill the dirty motherfucker!" shouted somebody else.

Everybody stormed out of their rooms and started yelling and chasing the monkey around the pool. None of them had been involved in the poststructuralist riots four chapters ago, although they all looked exactly the same as those rioters down to the shape of the nose, the diameter of the nostrils, and the elasticity of the deconstruction.

The monkey explodes.

This throws everybody out of sync. They don't know what to do.

They explode.

The motel explodes.

But somehow the motel retains its scaffolding and reconstructs itself *in extenso*.

It explodes again.

The manager slinks out of the flames and wonders what the hell is going on and he explodes.

The sun explodes. But not the moon.

Solar flares attack the earth, razing it from pole to pole, and the Blue Swallow Motel is the only thing left, preserved by a containment field bestowed upon it by friendly god particles.

The manager, burning, tries to turn the motel into a slave plantation. Frederick Douglass intervenes and bashes in the manager's skull with a hunk of asphalt torn from the road.

Only Douglass remains.

He gives a speech and the speech explodes. He starts over and the speech explodes again. He applies mindfulness to the situation and takes calculated breaths and starts over one more time and gets about five seconds into the speech before it explodes.

Thoughts explode before they are born. Before their parents and their grandparents are born.

The void explodes. The Lacanian Real a.k.a. the Dark Hypotenuse explodes.

Employing an uncanny will to power, Douglass psychokinetically recreates the Lacanian Real a.k.a. the Dark Hypotenuse, then retires to the motel. He can't remember what room he's staying in, and he doesn't want to ask the manager, because everybody knows the manager doesn't like black people. Plus he murdered the manager. So he strides up to a door and kicks it in.

Splinters spray across the uncured mattress.

He enters the room and the alabaster walls crumble into soot.

The entire Blue Swallow Motel mimics the pretense.

The air vaporizes.

Douglass can't breathe. He realizes why.

He got too close to the Lacanian Real a.k.a. the Dark Hypotenuse. Not only that: he recreated it.

That's what happens.

Watch any David Lynch movie.

Time and again: *the grimace of the Real.*

The impossible. The undifferentiated. That without fissure. That which is beyond (or beneath, or between) language.

As Lacan himself says: "The domain of whatever subsists outside of symbolization."

CHAPTER 86

I like what I did in the last chapter. Let's keep going down this road. Here's my favorite chapter from *Freud: The Penultimate Biography*:

CHAPTER 18

The government approached a famous movie director and asked if he would fake the moon landing for them.

"Fuck no."

The government approached the famous director again and encouraged him to fake that moon landing.

"Get the fuck outta here."

The government approached the famous director again and said c'mon really you should do this.

"All right fine," said the director. "I'll need some scotch-light screens and bean-splinters and some more fancy something-or-others. But I want to shoot it on the moon and I get to pick my own actors. For the lead, my gut instinct says Kirk Douglas, but my gut always tells me to go with Kirk, capiche? Now that I've thought about it a little though I'm thinking, like, I don't know, Moses Gunn or something."

"Moses Gunn? What was he in?"

"He's black."

They took him to the moon. On the way there the director asked a government official why they wanted to fake a landing.

"We don't want the Russians to see what we're doing up there. We're doing things on the moon."

"I guess I don't care. That seems like a good reason I guess. There could be anything going on up there.

Probably you're making pornos up there or some-thing but what do I care. Some pornos are pretty good."

The director went to the East Bay with the actors and they all crammed into an EVA pod and he told them how they were going to shoot this damned thing. He could smell Moses Gunn's breath. The actor's skin smelled funny, too. He made a face.

"White people smell just as funny to us," Gunn noted.

The director said he knew that and decided there wasn't enough room, so they got out of the pod and just walked freely around the bay as the director told them what to expect in terms of blocking and all that and then he handed out the script.

There were some off-the-cuff rewrites. One of the actors didn't like how they were all supposed to bound across the surface of the moon like inflated air-monkeys. Other actors worried about lighting and more real-world issues such as the flow of oxygen into spacesuits. Gunn didn't care about anything as long as he got paid. With a veteran's social finesse, the director attended to everybody's needs and they shot the footage and it all went pretty well.

The cameramen shot things in slow motion to convey a sense of low gravity even though in reality that wasn't how people would move on the moon; they'd move normal-like but with more featheriness and they'd go up and down and so forth. But people on earth expected moonwalkers to move in a certain slow-like way so that's how they shot it.

On the ride home the government official told the famous director it was a good thing he did that. Now he could go and make whatever kinds of movies he wanted, for the rest of his life, and the government wouldn't interfere or kill him.

"Do you really think you would have killed me? I don't think you would have."

The government official said well maybe not but we'll never know. Anyway that's some good moon footage you shot up there on the moon and we really appreciate it and so forth.

That night, after Vespers, the director went out for a drink with his wife. They sat at a table near the ocean and the moon loomed overhead like a death wish. Moonlight cascaded across the water from the horizon to the beach and seemed to spill into their wine glasses. They drank the most expensive bottle of Pinot Grigio the restaurant had to offer and then ordered another bottle plus two servings of sorbet.

CHAPTER 87

(NOTE: Don't get hung up on numbers. Numerology is for numerologists and other deranged occultists. There are 64 chapters in *Freud: The Penultimate Biography* so there's a one in 64 chance that the chapter from *Freud* I cited in the last chapter of *Nietzsche: The Unmanned Autohagiography* is my favorite chapter from *Freud*. You and I both want me to finish the book at this point and I'm moving really fast now so I just opened a copy of *Freud: The Penultimate Biography* to a random page and that's what went in chapter 86 of *Nietzsche: The Unmanned Autohagiography*. Remember, qua Reich: "This is not a book. It is an algorithm." Plus, I have to go to the bathroom again and refill my wine glass.)

CHAPTER 88

Here's my favorite chapter from *Hitler: The Terminal Biography*. Unlike my favorite chapters from *Freud: The Penultimate Biography* and *Douglass: The Lost Autobiography*, I have revised this one slightly so that it more effectively interlaces with the content of *Nietzsche: The Unmanned Autohagiography*:

CHAPTER 59

Recently, I gave a free, pro bono seminar for writers. I didn't want to but my publisher made me. Information was delivered on a point-by-point basis in an Austrian German (trans. *Österreichisches Deutsch*) dialect. Here's a synopsis. I have translated it into English for the purposes of this book and my predominantly English-speaking readership:

1. Bleep.

2. Bleep.

3. Don't use writing as an excuse to embody a geometry of sloth.

4. Take a shower. Tuck in your shirt. Comb your hair. Brush your teeth. You there. Yes, you. And you. You too. All of you. Good. Good. Good. Good.

5. Forget about the gym for now. Focus on diet. Eat one less meatball sandwich per day. We'll

start hitting the gym when you lose some weight and your muscles can breathe. The muscles need to remember that they exist, if only in an attenuated, wraithlike state.

6. Do not touch me. Ever. Assume my mind-body apparatus is off-limits. Pretend the apparatus is equipped with a default restraining order. I'm happy to sign books but keep your distance.

7. If you haven't already, check out my latest books, *The Kyoto Man*, a novel published by Raw Dog Screaming Press, and *Diegeses*, a collection of novelettes published by Anti-Oedipus Press. They're not my best work but they're all right.

8. Bleep!

9. Chloroplast.

10. Alois Villafuerte has eaten, like, eight lemon bars at this point. He can't stop. Also he drank too many espressos and he's having heart palpitations. He doesn't know what to do.

11. "Jouissance serves no purpose (*ne sert à rien*). ... Where there is being, infinity is required ... There's no such thing as a sexual relationship ... Stupidity nevertheless has to be nourished. Is everything we nourish thereby stupid? No. But it has been demonstrated that to nourish

oneself is part and parcel of stupidity ... What is at stake in analytic discourse is always the following—you give a different reading to the signifiers that are enunciated (*ce qui s'énonce de signifiant*) than what they signify ... The cosmic theory of knowledge or world view has always made a big deal of the famous example of smoke that cannot exist without fire ... Smoke can just as easily be the sign of a smoker. And, in essence, it always is. There is no smoke that is not a sign of a smoker. Everyone knows that, if you see smoke when you approach a deserted island, you immediately say to yourself that there is a good chance there is someone there who knows how to make fire. Until things change considerably, it will be another man. Thus, a sign is not the sign of some thing, but of an effect that is what is presumed as such by a functioning of the signifier" (Lacan 3, 10, 12, 14, 37, 49).

12. No Q & A.

CHAPTER 89

As the ride comes to a gentle end ... the Ferris Wheel accelerates from its usual speed of 1.5 mph to 60 mph within the span of 10 seconds, as if a teenager suddenly stepped on the gas. And yet the control panel remains untouched. All of the riders—parents and children, husbands and wives, boyfriends and girlfriends, people who have nobody, people who have never been born and have been dead for millennia—scream like hellions as they fly out of their capsules into the sky. Gravity ignores them. They keep going up and up and up until the alien atmosphere sets them aflame and explodes them like fireworks, one soft, indifferent pop after another.

CHAPTER 90

This is the trippy stargate sequence of the book wherein a repressed Bowmanesque journeyman enters the dragon and defeats Kareem Abdul-Jabbar in a knife fight on a midnight rooftop before growing elderly and becoming a twenty-first-century übermensch. All events occur in an elusive fasttime as the camera fetishizes a wide-shut eye in EXTREME CLOSE-UP. Careful attention is paid to the meta-dynamics of the Human Stain.

CHAPTER 91

There are no mustaches in space. Think about it.

CHAPTER 92

Apologies for chapter 91. That chapter wasn't worthy of absurdist theater, let alone a trippy stargate sequence.

There's no excuse for chapter 91.

Let's try again. More wine, darling. Thank you. Thanks. Ok. No. I'm barely shaking anymore. Yes. Yes. I think so. Yes. No. Yes.

CHAPTER 93

Here's a transcript from the first outtake for a commercial that a drunk Orson Welles did for Paul Masson wine:

Director [*offscreen*]: "Action please … Action Orson, please."

Welles [*delivers a languid, ten-second-long Kubrickian stare to the camera; then, slurring his words*]: "D'just … do anything?"

Director: "Sorry. Cut."

During the outtake, two stony, sharp-dressed French actors across the table from Welles observe him like a museum exhibit ("Orson").

CHAPTER 94

All films are fantasy films because nothing ever happens that way. All films are science fiction films because of the technologies used to make them and the technologies of the Human Stain (any extension of the body, ranging from a primitive bone-tool to a space-going nuclear warhead, is a technology). All films are horror films because it's scary to be alive, diegetically and non-diegetically. Hence the nature of our cultural existence is quite speculative in addition to being definitively cinematic. You understand.

CHAPTER 95

Most of my dreams involve making plans to get some wine, but my plans are deferred at every turn as I nego-tiate oneiric interlopers and battle certain manifestations of my anxieties and insecurities. I've never had a drink in a dream—I'm always sober in spite of my best efforts. It's just as well. My ex-wife doesn't exist in my dreams, so there's nobody to take me to the hospital when I get the DTs and vomit uncontrollably.

CHAPTER 96

"The hallowed barnacles of tomorrow are nothing like the oinking seagulls of futurity." —DONOVAN OGG

CHAPTER 97

Mise en abyme.

A man in a frock coat enters and staggers towards an open tomb on the opposite end of the stage. Halfway there, a trap door swallows him.

Somewhere in the bowels of the theater, the man is digested amid a weirdly harmonic musical score of hysterical shrieks and consternating tubas.

Finally, the tomb spits his body into the audience like chewed-up gristle, inciting a disposable riot. Ushers die first. All of the women, children, and actors get away.

CHAPTER 98

Deep depression in this moment.

We know it will pass, but sometimes it's unbearable.

It happens for an abundance of reasons. Hangovers. Failure to produce good art. Not making new memories. Living entirely on a diet of mnemonic afterburn.

So forth.

There's nobody at the University, in Dreamfield, or on the plateau of our collective innerspace who can help us. Ex-spouses only indulge us because they don't want our children to be sad if we die.

Life is a chronic exercise in exorcizing the feeling of melancholy and loneliness from our sensorium. The only thing that keeps us going is that every moment eventually collapses into the next.

"We won't always feel this way," we tell ourselves.

CHAPTER 99

Students who know how to properly deploy a semicolon in their essays invariably get As.

This makes sense.

The semicolon isn't like other articles of punctuation, which pale in comparison. Unless you use it to separate items in a list, one or more of which includes a comma, a semicolon functions exactly like a period; the only reason to use it at all is to join two sentences that are related in some way (e.g., this sentence). Together the dot and the comma amount to a perspicacious article of punctuation, and most people—regardless of age, class, race, gender, creed, etc.—can neither negotiate nor enact perspicacity as it relates to writing, identity, or life in general.

The problem is Priority.

If we believed less in God and more in semicolons, we would be edging closer to utopia than dystopia. Hence religion equates with Hell and punctuation with Heaven. Once again, you understand.

CHAPTER 100

It's chapter 100! That's twice my age.

I have a better body than Friedrich Wilhelm Nietzsche. Much better. At 50, my body is in the best shape it's ever been. Consider my strongest suits: rumblestrip obliques, bowling-ball shoulders, teardrop thighs, a vascularity like Schiaparelli's maps of Mars—no 50-year-old that I've ever met has outdone these features, and as I mentioned in chapter 12, I always linger between 8-12% body fat.

Nietzsche wasn't fat, but he wasn't in good shape, and he didn't lift weights. He was probably upset all the time. Same with Kafka. Same with nearly every pre-Schwarzenegger human being.

Weak, unexercised bodies render bad emotional dispositions, diseased organs, and shitty karma.

Similarly, one of my many out-of-shape editors is always in a bad mood and takes everything personally because he's fat and eats the wrong things (viz., non-whole foods and not enough greens). Recently, he edited a book I wrote about Alfred Bester's science-fiction masterwork *Tiger! Tiger!* (a.k.a. *The Stars My Destination*) in which I meta-referentially adopt the tone and voice of Bester, who variously made fun of science-fiction authors for being "empty people who have failed as human beings. As a class they are lazy, irresponsible, immature. They are incapable of producing contemporary fiction because they know nothing about life, cannot reflect life, and have no adult comment to make about life. They are silly childish people who have taken refuge in science fiction where they can establish their own arbitrary rules about reality to suit their own inadequacy. And like most neurotics, they cherish the delusion that they're 'special'" (434).

Bester bashed science-fiction readers in a similar vein, and "I" endorsed his stance, arguing that Herman Melville's *Moby-Dick* and James Joyce's *Ulysses* "might as well have been written by an alien from another dimension: the depth of Melville's allusions alone is entirely lost on twenty-first century generations" (Wilson, *Alfred* 34). Insecure and anxious, my editor took such assertions personally. In this case—as in most cases throughout the manuscript— he offered no useful feedback; rather, he included this note in the margin: "I've never read Melville or Joyce and I'm doing just fine."

He's not doing fine. He can't stop overeating, and like Nietzsche, he won't go to the gym. Every day, he gets softer and angrier.

I keep telling the editor that he'll feel better and develop a much healthier perspective if he cleans up his diet and starts doing core workouts just two to three times a week for 30 minutes. It's so easy. Just count your calories. I eat approximately 2,000 calories a day with macros that amount to about 200 grams of protein (mostly chicken and fish), 200 grams of carbs (mostly rice), and 50 grams of healthy fats (entirely egg yolks, avocado, and/or flaxseed butter). For a 6'5" male who works out 60-90 minutes per day five days per week, that's too few calories, but I like to stay Joker-lean, especially as I get older.

CHAPTER 101

Christianity today is not the crummy dis-ease that it was for Herr Nietzsche in the nineteenth century. The organized Christian religion, however, like all religions, and like all beliefs, remains a cancer, a virus, a plague—a *movement* by Little Men to control people with infinite hammers of Anxiety and Insecurity. The only reason the movement doesn't die is because people are afraid of death. I can't blame them. I want there to be an afterlife in the sky, but I can't bring myself to disavow biological reality and favor desire over truth. Like Nietzsche, I'm a slave to my life's thesis: *Belief is the end of reason and the beginning of evil.*

CHAPTER 102

The idea that certain people will live forever by way of their work or deeds is a myth, as is the notion that, say, a place will never die.

My father thinks America is immortal. His patriotism knows no ends, and anything that threatens his purview either doesn't exist or deserves to be punished.

Logic has no place in this place.

"I'm a patriot," says my father. "I don't care what you or anybody says about it. America will live forever."

I say: "Talk to me in 1,000 years. Better yet, talk to me in 10,000 years, or 100,000 years, or a few million years. Humanity will be long gone. We're too stupid and too selfish and too hedonistic to live. Time, on the other hand, is neither stupid nor selfish nor hedonistic. Time is brainless, emotionless, careless, relentless. Unlike us, time will never stop. It will keep going until it kills everything in the Universe. Then it will kill the Universe."

"And then?" says my father.

"Then? There will be no then. No then and no now. No yesterday either."

"There must be something. Where will time live?"

"The only place it can live. The place it has always lived best and truest. The place that lives in the shadow of the burning sun."

"What place is that, son?"

CHAPTER 103

The Blue Swallow Motel hangs from the iron jaw of futurity like a slave on a cross. The place smells bad and the place looks bad. The sun is a wooden nickel in the sky.

There's a dead monkey lying on the pavement outside of Room 6. It walked out of the room and died of sadness a few hours ago. Let's watch it decompose for awhile as we consider what invoked mortal sadness in this poor hairy man-thing.

[*Space for reflection.*]

There. Now go to the next page. I've finally found my stride and I'm good for at least 100 more chapters. Yes. No.

CHAPTER 104

Are you a worm or a god? Your answer to this question—and your exegesis of the answer—will solarize everything that you lack and embody, everything that you reap and sow, everything that you see and misperceive.

CHAPTER 105

WRITING TIP: Go to a café in a different country where you don't understand the language. Sameness is the Stain's dominant characteristic, but this "foreign" world of seemingly dynamic language and peoples will trick you into thinking that the world and its peoples are themselves dynamic and interesting, thus providing more dynamic and interesting content to write about (despite the absolute nonexistence of the content). This is difficult for me since I can speak and read all Romance and Germanic languages, so I have to go to Russia or Eastern Europe to get my Humanity Fix, however delusional it may be. Remember that our delusions scaffold reality and perception, ideology and onotology. Neither subjectivity nor objectivity can elude the forces of our idiocy and unselfawareness. The best we can do is acknowledge the moon's affection.

CHAPTER 106

Loving yourself is the worst thing. Hate yourself. Then I might begin to like you.

CHAPTER 107

I mentioned that I have a superpower in chapter 39. Go reread it and come back.

Are you back?

I should add that the superpower applies to every aspect of objective and subjective reality, including the University, the Blue Swallow Motel, Pangea, all of my dreams and your dreams and the dreams of extinct species, etc., etc.

I don't want anything from anywhere or anybody.

The only beef I have is with the future: somewhere in the that clump of temporal fabric, my death awaits me like a raptor in the bushes.

If I want anything, it's only to project my personal history onto eternity and crystallize it in amber.

CHAPTER 108

As I opined in *Hitler: The Terminal Biography*, one should always judge a book by its cover, but not the cover alone. The first sentence must be taken into account.

Everything else beyond the first sentence of a book constitutes superfluity and similitude, ego and ennui. Novels in particular are subject to the rule. "The first sentence should be sufficient and contain the seeds, the sprouts, the trunk and the leaves and the distant stump of the entire narrative," I say in *Hitler*. "If it doesn't, it's a bad novel" (101-02).

Consider the first sentence of, say, let's see … Hold on.

I'm going to run to my library and pick out a few titles. Last year, I bought the four-bedroom condo next door to my three-bedroom condo and that's where I keep all my books. Be right back.

I'm back.

Consider the first sentence of Herman Melville's *Pierre* (1852): "There are some strange summer mornings in the country, when he who is but a sojourner from the city shall early walk forth into the fields, and be wonder-smitten with the trance-like aspect of the green and golden world" (3).

That's actually a bad example. And a bad novel. It might be the literary equivalent of *Plan 9 from Outer Space* (1959). How about the first sentence of Dempow Torishima's *Sisyphean* (2013)?

In stable orbit above a congealed accretion disc in the depths of galactic space, there swarmed untold millions of corporations, who together formed the immense, nimbotranslucent corpuspheres of which an archipellagolopolis was composed. In the midst of their jostlings were two consolidated corporations—Gyo the Intercessor and Ja the Vigilant—who together formed a stately, gourdlike shape over ten thousand shares in diameter. (7)

This is better than Melville's effort, and the sentence resonates with me—vivid, bombastic descriptions suit my aesthetic sensibilities and *modes de vie*—but objectively speaking, it amounts to Trying Too Hard with regard to the surreal, cognitively estranging future in which Torishima sets his novel. Besides, the sentence was translated from Japanese into English by Daniel Hiddleston, and translation always entails loss. What we're reading is more of an interpretation. The same goes for all of the books by Nietzsche that I've cited in *Nietzsche: The Unmanned Autohagiography*, but that's for your benefit—I only read the New High German versions of his work.

Let's do this again.

For diversity's sake, look at the first sentence of Ralph Ellison's *Invisible Man* (1952): "I am an invisible man" (3).

No. Try H.G. Wells's *The Invisible Man* (1897): "The stranger came early in February, one wintry day, through a biting wind and a driving snow, the last snowfall of the year, over the down, walking from Bramblehurst railway station, and carrying a little black portmanteau in his thickly gloved hand" (1).

There's ample descriptive rhetoric here that gestures towards the mystery of the novel's antagonist in the context of a Shakespearean Winter of Discontent. But I want more. I always want more. As I used to tell my ex-wife (siphoning Bond): "The world is not enough."

Virginia Woolf's *The Waves* (1931)—here's the first sentence: "The sun had not yet risen" (3).

I don't like that sentence. And I don't remember *The Waves*. I often say I love Virginia Woolf, but I think that's a lie.

Let's pretend the dead monkey from chapter 103 wrote a book. What would the first sentence be? Could it really be any worse than most of the books that have ever been or will be written?

It occurs to me that I may have tried and failed at this experiment in *Hitler: The Terminal Biography* as well as *Freud: The Penultimate Biography* and *Douglass: The Lost Autobiography*. My compulsion for redundancy never gets old and never goes away. If there's one thing addiction has taught me, it's that I never learn, viz., I never care enough about something to remember anything.

CHAPTER 109

What time is it? How long has it been since I went to the bathroom and had a slash?

The feeling of having to go to the bathroom has completely escaped me. It didn't even occur to me to go when I went to my condo-library in the previous chapter.

By my reckoning, at some point during the last thirty minutes, that filled-to-the-rim compulsion, that biological anxiety transformed into the abject itself. It's outside of my body, the feeling. Hence it no longer exists, and it may never return from the grave. The IV of Malbec at my bedside won't save me.

Julia Kristeva's theory of the abject is a touchstone for this sort of nonsense. All theory is nonsense literature, good for nothing but idle scholarly bling. At best, it's good for increasing the size of one's lexicon and the scope of one's imagination. Ludovico scholars don't like when I convey this truth, but nobody likes truth in any form, package, or mask.

What was I saying? Let's reconnoiter.

Feces (metaphorical and actual).

Anxiety (actual only).

Wine (12 ccs every 60 seconds).

Kristeva ("The abject has only one quality of the object—that of being opposed to I" [230]).

Right.

Now we know who we are and what we're doing again, even if my conceptual armada will never fall prey to the scapegoat of your latent desires.

CHAPTER 110

That last chapter wasn't written by me. The alcohol wrote it.

One should never write drunk. Drinking is for revising and polishing texts. I am the best stylist I can be when I'm full of poison.

Dreams are the bank vault of human memory. See Jung. The vault is locked, however, and nobody has the combination to open it, to storm inside, to commandeer the Golden Cogs and unleash their hoary secrets. Even Nietzsche lacked the combination.

Where does this leave us?

Nietzsche is the hinge for the philosophy of Ancients and the schizosophy of Futurists.

If this seminal madman can't bust down the door and eat all the chickens, nobody can.

CHAPTER 111

I keep nodding off. I think I'm passed out.

How did the Rat Pack do it?

"You're not drunk if you can lie on the floor without holding on," Dean Martin once quipped (Wells, "Here's").

Frank Sinatra drank a bottle of scotch a day until he was 80, then switched to wine when his doctors told him that he needed to stop (Johnson). He died two years later at 82 of a double heart attack after suffering Zarathustrian dementia brought on by antidepressants (Jacob).

Yes. No.

Invariably, I can tell I'm dreaming in my dreams, and I remind myself constantly. "You're dreaming," I remind myself. "It's a dream. This is a dream. Remember. Remember where you are. Recognize what's happening to you." I do this in bad oneiric situations. I do it in good ones, too. If things are going well, I don't want to be too depressed when I awake. If things are going poorly, I don't want to be too depressed in the dream itself.

The status of reality or consciousness is another matter. When I'm awake and alive, I can never confirm these things to be true.

CHAPTER 112

In the final scene of *Nietzsche's Kisses*, Lance Olsen reverts to the beginning of Nietzsche's life and depicts his birth. "Look at Little Fritz," says the midwife who delivers him. "He is kissing the future" (244).

CHAPTER 113

In *I Am Dynamite! A Life of Nietzsche*, Sue Prideaux brings her discussion to a close with a melodramatic paragraph that refers to the title of her book and responds to a mad maxim that appears in the chapter entitled "Why I Am Fatality" of Nietzsche's *Ecce Homo*: "I am not a man—I am dynamite" (96). "Hearts shaped by history sink at the prophecy," writes Prideaux.

> But only in our imagination darkened by the long shadow of hindsight is this the cry of a man wanting to unleash evil upon the world. Rather, it sounds the triumphant call of the man who blasted a tunnel through his own age's heavy indifference to the consequences of the death of God, opening the way for audacious Argonauts of the spirit to reach new worlds. (381)

Many of Nietzsche's dominant themes are effectively invoked in this paragraph (e.g., history, divination, retrospection, good vs. evil, God's death, Greek mythology, and the quest for genuine innovation), rendering the paragraph's melodrama an issue of entropy and scholarship more than emotion and style.

CHAPTER 114

Here's R.J. Hollingdale's final sentiment in *Nietzsche: The Man and his Philosophy*:

> He was to be called "holy"—and, rather more frequently, "unholy"—for a century after his death. Today all this is, or should be, a part of the past: "Nietzscheanism" is as dead as "Wagnerism," and what we are left with is not a doctrine that might be preached and stand in need of defense but a human individual, an artist in language of great skill and power, and a philosopher of compelling insight and strictness of principle; we are left with the man and his philosophy. His life and thought were both in a sense "experiments," and insofar as they were both carried through to a logical end they are self-justified and require no defending. (254)

Now pretend that Nietzsche was really not a Native American and revisit everything that has been said in our Little Book. Observe how your perception of this autohagiographic landscape molts like snakeskin.

In the next chapter, I will discuss how I have forgotten what I'm doing and reflect on what this book *does*. What it *is* doesn't matter. Only actions can produce reactions.

CHAPTER 115

Hello! I've forgotten what this book is about.

This always happens.

I mean, it's about Nietzsche, kind of, but beyond this topical marker, the book doesn't seem to be about much of anything or anybody. That said, there are distinct themes, voices, sleights of hand, etc., all of which we might call "deliberate" and "purposeful," if not "methodical," "systematized," and "altogether preemptive."

There's even character and plot development in some areas. This is the problem, you see.

CHAPTER 116

The news is a cultural extension of collective desire and anxiety, and the news loves destruction, death, and coordinated nudity. Without the news, there would be no viable stories to tell. Hence the following narrative:

Mother, Father, and I travel to Austria under duress. Dad is mostly a cyborg at this point, with artificial organs and a weaponized exoskeleton, but since his third retirement—this time from driving a schoolbus—he hasn't known what to do with himself. We flew to Berlin on a redeye at his vociferous behest. He gesticulated and barked loudly at the flight attendants for peanuts and scotch as clouds exploded like dirigibles and threatened to take us down. He only killed one passenger. The passenger deserved it, but Dad didn't use any of his tech. He strangled him in the lavatory and stuffed the corpse into the undercarriage of a beverage cart.

At the hotel, Mom puts our clothes away and Dad drinks all of the miniatures in the refrigerator. In less than two hours, he and I are supposed to visit clients, but I refused to go, fearful of Nazis.

"Nazis are a myth, son," Dad assures me. "They're historical artifacts, anyway. They can't get you from the past. If they get you, it'll be in the future, after they're born again. Cycle of life, like."

Dad never talks like that. His tech is taking over again. The Singularity will ingest him, I suspect, by nightfall.

He threatens to "do something" and Mom threatens to call a brownshirt from the front desk "if you do anything."

"Calm down, darling. Son? We have clients to see."

"You keep saying that. What clients? What's our job?"

"No funny business now. Do you hear me, boy? This is real business. This isn't another one of your artsy fartsy puppet shows. Get your shit together. We gotta land these sauerkrauts *today*. We're leaving in five minutes."

Dad gets in the shower to wash his bones. He never comes out, and nobody ever sees him again.

"Where's Dad?"

Mom collapses like a marionette whose puppeteer has abandoned her.

"Mom?"

The hotel room unfolds like an accordion in a VR simulation. In the end, I'm naked, pacing back and forth in front of a towering, roaring fireplace that looks like it belongs in *Citizen Kane*'s Xanadu. The mise is black-and-white now, and Mom is hiding beneath the covers of the Victorian bed that occupies an adjacent dining room. I know she's worried about the dirigible ride this afternoon. Surely the dirigible will explode—dirigibles explode in this diegesis with the same regularity as clouds—but somehow, I will devise a way to relieve her anxiety. I just need to keep thinking. The more I think, the less I am.

CHAPTER 117

My mental health is declining rapidly.

Over the course of the two-or-so hours it took me to get to the 117th chapter, a lot has happened in my head, most of it bad.

I'm really writing this dumb book because I'm afraid of the Kubrick book that I should be writing right now. Here's my working thesis:

The futurist trilogy (and its "artificial" posthumous addendum) tells an implicit, subtextual meta-story from beginning to end about the Kubrickian filmind's evolving consciousness. This meta-story hinges on the flows of desire and the sublime, mediatized, patho-logical dreamworlds constructed by an increasingly aggressive technoculture.

The futurist trilogy consists of *Dr. Strangelove, 2001: A Space Odyssey*, and *A Clockwork Orange*. The addendum is *A.I. Artificial Intelligence*, directed by Steven Spielberg, who took the baton from Kubrick after his death in 1999. Kubrick worked on the script for almost twenty years before his death, but even if he had lived, he wanted Spielberg to direct it. Spielberg's artistry, Kubrick knew, was a better fit for the narrative content and visual spec-tacle of *A.I.*

Like Friedrich Nietzsche, there's too much scholarship on Stanley Kubrick. I'm worried about establishing and sustaining a unique line of critical flight.

I wrote a 10,000-word proposal for Auteur Publishing (an imprint of Liverpool University Press) to be part of their new Kubrick Studies series. The proposal sounds great, and the publisher loved it, but it's all bullshit. I don't know what I'm doing. I never do. I've read and taken notes on every book ever published on Kubrick and his oeuvre, including hundreds of articles and related material. I have a cogent thesis and I've already done the hard legwork, scaffolding every chapter with textual fiberoptics and beams of support.

I will fail. There's no way not to be redundant vis-à-vis Kubrick.

More wine?

No. Not this time.

Yes. This time. Every time.

I really just need to work out for a few hours. My endorphins are stronger than ethanol. Three giant sets consisting of weighted dips, dumbbell bench presses, and cable crosses will straighten me out and evaporate this heavy velvet brainfog.

I always worry about the Next Day. Literally, it means I'll have to negotiate the DTs and either choose to drink or not to drink in order to feel better and stop shaking like a leaf in a storm.

Psychologically, the Next Day means I'll have to negotiate new fictions that plague and play on my mindscreen.

Existentially, the Next Day means I'll have to come up with another excuse not to drown myself in the lake across the street.

"Don't walk into that old lake," I tell myself.

It's really a dare.

My careworn psyche hurts more than my physical discomfort, although they're connected, and they feed off of one another. Wherever you go, there you are. But I need to get away from you.

You will be the death of me.

CHAPTER 118

All of my biographies are pretenses whereby I can tell you about my own life and authorship. That's what everybody's interested in.

I can't remember if I mentioned it in *Nietzsche: The Unmanned Autohagiography*, but Hitler, Freud, Douglass, and Nietzsche have all been extensively biographized by many other capable scholars, all of whom have written about themselves.

I know what you want. You're here to learn about me.

As a person, I live a fabulously boring life.

Like most Dreamfielders, I never go anywhere else, and I *never* diverge from the monotony of my daily routine. My real life is in my head and unfolds in my fiction. That's why I write so many goddamn books.

The only reason I'm on social media is to show my parents pics of my daughters (2% effort) and promote my books for my publishers (98% effort). Otherwise you'd never see me on Facebook, Twitter, or Instagram. These hellholes are little more than gaping symptoms of the Human Stain, but it's hard for authors to reach potential readers these days. Readers are dying en masse whereas "authors" are replicating like Old World Catholics.

There are many tactics whereby I promote my work on these platforms. One is to cite interesting apothegms in order to pique the interest of readers.

Consider the apothegm I cited in chapter 21, "I write because I'm weak," which I attributed to *Douglass: The Lost Autobiography*. The apothegm turns the longstanding notion that "the pen is mightier than the sword" on end, a tactic I deploy all the time (viz., say the diametric opposite of accepted conventions and back it up with compelling, rhetorically attractive horseshit). Our media-saturated, science-fictionalized world has seen the pen become as mighty as a sun-dried worm, but that's another story. My point is that this apothegm does not derive from *Douglass: The Lost Autobiography*. Nor does it derive from *Freud: The Penultimate Biography* or *Hitler: The Terminal Biography*. It came to me one day while I was promoting the biographies online. It synched with the thematic m.o. of the trilogy, so I attributed it to one of them and posted it alongside the cover for *Douglass: The Lost Autobiography*, beautifully designed by the multi-talented Matthew Revert. Check it out:

I do this all the time. Most of the apothegms I quote aren't requotes from my former books. Again, I don't remember my books once I'm done with them. I'm responsible for my actions. To some extent, I'm even responsible for my beliefs and my words. But nobody can blame me for my mnemonic shortcomings.

Nietzsche had the same problem …

CHAPTER 119

Ecce Homo constitutes a meta-autohagiographical coda to Nietzsche's oeuvre wherein he reflects on the implications of his philosophy and books while simultaneously aping and lionizing himself. The voice and tone of the coda belong to a cartoon.

In the Christian bible, Roman governor Pontius Pilate uttered "*Ecce homo*" when he presented a mauled, bloodied Jesus Christ to the people of Judaea for judgment (105). The utterance means: "Behold the man."

October/November 1888: Nietzsche composes *Ecce Homo* in Turin, Italy.

January 1889: Nietzsche witnesses a horse being flogged in Piazza Carlo Alberto, tries to save it, ruptures the wrong bundle of synapses, and goes insane. Thereafter he is institutionalized for over a decade.

August 25, 1900: Nietzsche dies of pneumonia.

Chapter titles in *Ecce Homo* include "Why I Am So Wise," "Why I Am So Clever," and "Why I Write Such Great Books." The last chapter is "Why I Am Fatality," which includes the best sentence ever written by any author. You know it: "I am not a man—I am dynamite" (96).

Ecce Homo contains equal portions of megalomania, satire, and self-reflexivity, all of it enacted with a kind of showbiz hysteria. Many scholars have said that it is a work of madness, but Nietzsche knew what he was doing.

CHAPTER 120

I was once addicted to an opioid called kratom (*mitragyna speciose*). It's a leaf you can order online. I made tea with it and drank the tea day and night, waking up in the early morning to have a cup so I could get back to sleep. Sometimes we get depressed, lonely, and misanthropic. Kratom yanks these feelings out of us like a Caerbannog rabbit from a magician's hat.

Online, kratom is marketed in a variety of ways, ranging from a holistic mood regulator to a means of assuaging chronic pain and detoxing from heroin. It's illegal in some states, but we can get it in Dreamfield.

When I realized the degree of my addiction, I stopped taking kratom. Cold turkey. That's how I do everything. I'm either all-in or I'm all-out.

Withdrawal symptoms lasted for months, and I didn't sleep for weeks.

For a brief period, I was institutionalized and prescribed an anti-psychotic, among other drugs.

I remember sitting in the "nest area" with my fellow Looney Toons, shaking and starving (I hadn't eaten in weeks either). I continued to take notes on the biography I was writing at the time—apropos, *The Psychotic Dr. Schreber*—and at no time did I not know what I was doing.

CHAPTER 121

I mention *style* in several chapters that appear in *Nietzsche: The Unmanned Autohagiography*. Remember? See chapters

23, 28, and 113, for instance. Only when something becomes redundant does it become meaningful.

Kubrick's cinematic consciousness exhibits a style that makes everything else redundant. Violence, sublimity, sexuality, primitivism, the grotesque, the uncanny, "wargasm," doppelgängers, surrealism, ambiguity, techno-pathology, obsession, oneiricism, the futility of intelligence, the distrust of emotion—all of these basic Kubrickian monad's are subject to the hammer of the auteur's inimitable style.

CHAPTER 122

In *Violence*, Slavoj Žižek says: "Nietzsche was repeatedly reinvented throughout the twentieth century: the conservative-heroic proto-fascist Nietzsche became the French Nietzsche and then the cultural-studies Nietzsche" (151).

And now, in the twenty-first century, the post-real, hyper-mediatized, ultra-caricatured Nietzsche finally digs in his bootheels.

He is more cartoon than man now. As it should be.

In the end, we all become cartoons.

Cartoons can be infinitely reborn and resurrected.

Cartoons are always mad and never die.

CHAPTER 123

I'd like to say that there's some significance to the number 123. As I mentioned in chapter 55, my biofictional novel *Peckinpah: An Ultraviolent Romance* has 59 chapters, one for each year of the titular auteur's life, and the 59th chapter is a eulogy in the form of a prose poem.

There's none of that here, but meaning can be made by anybody. Desire always outmaneuvers reason, truth, and objectivity. Hence religion. I leave the number 123 in the hearts and minds of my capable readers. *The Shining*'s room 237 has been said to mean anything, everything, and nothing. Do likewise with the numeric character of this final chapter regarding the life and times of Friedrich Wilhelm Nietzsche.

I'm too drunk to write anymore.

Predictably, I remain highly functional, and I rue the morning. Doubtless the morning will see me shaking from the DTs, parrying the anxiety-films that explode onto my mindscreen, and slithering back onto the Wagon.

Everybody has a book living inside of them, as they say. Thanks for reading this one in any case. You did good. It's over now. You made it. Maybe I'll make it, too.

For more tips on how to write biographies, autobiographies, autohagiographies, and other fine infotaintments, please listen to my podcast on Spotify, "The Electromagnetic Earthfucker Hour," and sign up for my masterclass at this address:

WWW.MASTERCLASS.COM/D-HARLAN-WILSON-TEACHES-NITCH

Have I been understood? *The Dark Hypotenuse vs. the Culture Machine* ...

———◆———

ABORTED CHAPTERS

CHAPTER A

I'd like to take this opportunity to spray my readership with gunfire.

The death of the reader long preceded the death of the author. One wonders if the reader has ever been alive.

Refer to the hieroglyphic walls of Zarathustra's Cave for more details.

CHAPTER B

As a young author, I never understood why many old authors stopped writing. I thought I would write forever, and I was overconfident that I would acquire the infinite momentum that these lapsed elder statespeople failed to acquire themselves.

I understand them now.

After years and years of manipulating the Word, they saw the Code.

Once you see the Code, the Code imprints you, and you see Everything.

Once the Code imprints you and you see Everything, you belong to the Code, and the Code forever bullies you like a goofy, weak-looking preteen.

The only path to Unbelonging is to disconnect from the System altogether.

Ignoring the Code only gets you so far.

CHAPTER C

Welcome to the pleasure dome of another chapter! This one will be about holidays.

I despise holidays. Ritual of any kind is an insult to me, yet another insignia of the social construction inimical to the Human Stain. More importantly, most people are sad and depressed during holidays because it reminds them of loved ones who have died and/or they are not enjoying their shitty lives. When happy people say "Happy Holidays," they have accomplished one of the Stain's many selfish, narcissistic, unforgivable acts.

CHAPTER D

All of my writing is an exfoliation of death that operates precisely like the human colon, which rebuilds itself on a daily basis. That's why most people can be alcoholics for so long. You know.

CHAPTER E

Whenever an ad or commercial interrupts a show or film that I'm watching, I close my eyes so that I can't see the annoyance, and for good measure, I filibuster the annoyance with rhetorical *Sturm und Drang* so that I can't hear it. "Fuck you, Ad!" I bellow. "Fuck you, Commercial! Fuck you! Fuck you, you fuckin' Ad! Fuck you, you goddamn Commercial! I hate you! I hate you! Fuck you! Fuck you! Fuck you! Fuck you, you son of a bitch! Fuck you! I hate you! I hate you, goddamn it!" And so on in a prosaic, unceasing stream of white noise until the ad or commercial is over and I open my eyes.

I win; consumer-capitalism loses.

CHAPTER F

Give addicts who kill themselves a break. It's not about you, the kids, etc. No amount of love or promise matters. Only an addict cut from the same cog can understand that none of the dead partygoers were partygoers at all. Blame Inevitability. Blame the Human Stain.

CHAPTER G

I have enunciated or (re)written these two "mad maxims" on multiple occasions:

1. Poetry died with the modernists.
2. Poetry is something people do before they become real writers.

Fact is, the only reason I don't write poetry is because I don't have time; I had to give it up in graduate school when I was trying to produce fiction, criticism, and poetry on a daily basis while jockeying pedagogy with editing projects. Something had to go. As I've said before, I'm all-in or all-out, no matter what's at stake.

I started writing poetry in college, but I had to do it in secret. My fraternity brothers would have roasted me endlessly if they found out that I was composing stanzas. So I wrote stanzas on the sly, and I met with my poetry professor on the sly to discuss my output.

My first published poem was entitled "Warfare." I paid for it to be published in a predatory anthology called *A Moment in Time* in 1994.

My second published poem, "God," appeared in a University of Massachusetts-Boston student magazine named *Waterworks.* That was in 1995.

In 1998, my final published poem, "A Peck at My Door," composed at a Bed and Breakfast in Edinburgh, Scotland, appeared in the literary journal *Exile.* This two-stanza, slant-rhymed micro-epic regards the life and times of an evil pigeon, "one of many rodents that plagues the afterlife in the sky" (Wilson, "A Peck" 7). It's based on a pigeon that was staring at me outside a window of the B&B as I drank Nescafé and tried to think of something to put on paper.

Afterwards I wrote about 5,000 more poems and published none of them. Then I gave up.

Giving up is hard for me but I do it all the time. I give up my soul to the University every semester. I give up drinking at least once a week. I give up ideas every day. So forth.

My forte is literary and film criticism. I've gotten better at fiction over the years, and I started writing plays in 2014. Propelled by an obsessive-compulsive work ethic, a little imagination can go a long way. Whatever I write, though, is undergirded by my efforts to become a famous poet like Mike Myers' character in *So I Married an Ax Murderer* (1993), who drives a dirty convertible VW Karmann Ghia and presumably makes enough money doing public readings to live comfortably in San Francisco.

The best authors possess a deep-rooted poetic foundation and can see and hear the Code of language, composing syntax like musical notation. If nothing else, the best authors tried or wanted to be poets at one time, if only for an oneiric moment.

Fact is, I'm a big dummy, but qua Nitch, I work harder than almost everybody else who is alive, and for the most part, I succeed in overcoming my dire inadequacies.

CHAPTER F

Dreams are either meaningful or disposable. Subjectivity sets the terms of what amounts to endearment or inoperability. Right?

We're in the woods. My ex-wife climbs a tree and won't come down. She's afraid of me. She knows something I don't know.

"Come down here, wife," I intone.

"Ex-wife!" she reminds me.

"What's going on up there?"

"None of your business. I don't feel like pretending you exist today. Those are my feelings."

"Feelings?" I intone.

I escort my daughters into a stately log cabin where a committee of Administrators detain us. Most of these uncanny gentlemen have been plucked from Bruceploitation films. The contours of their ill-defined bodies emit a dull, seething corona.

My daughters scream as two suited g-men with goat heads drag them down the hallway and lock them in the wine cellar.

"Wine?" I intone.

Bald Administrators were disbarred years ago: their veined, gleaming skulls reveal too much about their aspirations for power. Nowadays, whoever has the highest forehead is the Man of the Crowd.

In addition to a high forehead, the Alpha is distinguished by a black turtleneck, teacup ears, and a feathered gray hairdo. I don't know what his body looks like even as I scrutinize it, but there's something about the angle of his jaw, the anvil of his heart.

"Father?" I intone.

The Administrators beat me with extendable batons and cuff me to a radiator next to a bar counter that glows from underneath. Then the Alpha casually slips behind the bar and asks who wants a martini.

Everybody does.

I peer around the radiator and eyeball the Alpha to indicate that he should make me a martini, too. Boozing in dreams threatens my waking sobriety and destabilizes my chi, according to my therapist, but I can't reach the benzos in my pocket to help me negotiate all of these provocations and violations against my expectations.

After everybody has been served, the Alpha obliges me. He only lets me take one sip before ordering the goatmen to pick me up and deposit me on a bed in an adjacent motel room.

"This looks like the Blue Swallow Motel," I observe.

The Alpha punches me in the face. "Stop doing what you're doing," he says.

"Ow! What am I doing? Jesus."

"You know what you're doing."

"No I don't. I'm sitting here. I'm getting beat up. I'm not drinking a martini. That's what I'm doing."

"Wake up."

"Fuck off."

"Look up."

"What?"

"Look up."

"What?"

"Look up."

"Up where?"

"Up there."

He clutches the handle of my jaw and cranks back my head like a lever.

In the ceiling, I see a vague screen embedded in a brown water stain. It's my mind's screen, and it's threatening the stability of the universe.

As you pass into the fold of my unconscious and become part of the Show, you feel as badly as I do about everything. Now you know the truth about a monkey's sadness.

CHAPTER G

While I favor Batfleck, all of the Batmans did a good job in their own aesthetic rights and historical contexts, including Adam West. I can't say the same thing for Mr. Bond. In the distant future, mark my words—where you fall on this issue will dictate who dies and who lives.

CHAPTER H

Alois Villafuerte is gonna scream as loud as he can for about 20 minutes, pausing only to refill his lungs with Dreamfield air, which is laced with manure and toxins that issue from the ersatz lake across the road from his condo. In this diegesis, the Blue Swallow Motel only exists as a figment of his imagination. Occasionally the motel materializes in a nightmare.

CHAPTER I

In this nightmare, Alois Villafuerte lets down his guard and goes on a drinking binge.

It's been awhile since he fell off the Wagon.

You wouldn't like him when he falls off the Wagon.

It starts out harmless enough. A friendly cocktail during Happy Hour on Friday.

By Sunday, Alois Villafuerte has to keep drinking to stave off the DTs.

Delirium tremens.

He hasn't worked out in days. It's too hard to lift weights. He forces himself to jog on the treadmill for two hours while drinking mimosas.

In the afternoon, he drinks four Kentucky Bourbon Ales. That night, he downs a jumbo musket of Malbec and a pint of obscure Russian vodka.

The DTs hit Alois Villafuerte like a mythological god's wrath as he awakens the next day into the horror of Anxiety Unbound. There's no booze in the condo. He lasts as long as he can, then drinks a bottle of Listerine to stop shaking and hallucinating and sweating and hyperventilating …

Repeat yesterday.

The next day, the DTs hit Alois Villafuerte like a mythological god's wrath as he awakens into the horror of Anxiety Unbound … again.

Again. Again. Again.

At some point, his body rejects further alcohol intake. Who knows what day it is.

Alois Villafuerte vomits involuntarily for 15 hours every 15 minutes. Then he must pace the hallways of his condo for another 15 hours, pausing every hour to make himself vomit because it temporarily displaces the Dread.

Alois Villafuerte counts the minutes of his sobriety as they unfold while staving off the dark fictions that play across his mindscreen. There is so much regret. There is too much fear.

Guilt and shame. Embarrassment. Waves of agony and heartache and evil-doing nostalgia.

Alois Villafuerte turns to an old Christian bible for emotional support and prays to God for help in spite of his resolute agnostic stance and outlook. Give me a message that will save me, prays Alois Villafuerte. He opens the bible to a random page and reads a line that he underlined as a child in Sunday School.

It's the last line in Job 17: "Shall we descend together into the dust?" (455).

24 hours later, Alois Villafuerte swallows an edible and manages to sleep for five hours. When he wakes up, he feels semi-normal again, but it will be at least 10 days until he straightens out psychologically, emotionally, etc.

Alois Villafuerte vows never to fall off the Wagon again, even though he knows the roads need work. The Wagon will hit potholes and surely throw him off. He requires more than one seat belt.

Alois Villafuerte's "support network" consists of his Unfamily, of his ex-wife and his daughters, the latter of whom are too young to understand broken dreams. It was his choice to drink that first drink. "We are who we choose to be," says the Green Goblin in *Spider-Man* (2002). But only villains deserve the rancor of this comic-book villainy.

CHAPTER J

No idea what to put here.

CHAPTER K

Here either.

CHAPTER L

Nietzsche proposed marriage to the Russian-born psycho-analyst and author Solomé on two occasions in 1882. She turned him down, but she probably wet his whistle a few times and let him eat her out.

Many biographers have posited that Nietzsche burned a candle for Solomé for the rest of his life. This candle may have contributed to the hammer of madness that slammed down on him in 1889, they say.

After Nietzsche's death in 1900, hundreds of unsent letters were found beneath the floorboards of his bedroom in his sister Elizabeth's Weimar home. He spent the first part of his post-breakdown life in a Basel asylum, then his mother looked after him until she died in 1897. Nietzsche spent his final years under the care of Elizabeth. He never said a word. Was this 11-year stint of aphasic incapacitation an elusive stunt? More curiously, none of the letters were addressed to Solomé. Most of them were written to one "Frau Grendelmeister," whose identity remains a mystery, and they can only be accessed via the Nietzsche Archives at the University of Arts-Gatlinburg in the Speculative Collections Library. For whatever reason, the curators of the Nietzsche Estate will not release them for publication.

The last letter, dated two days before his death on August 23, is a 500,000-word revision and update of *The Birth of Tragedy*.

The second to last letter, dated the day before on August 22, is much shorter.

"Dear Frau Grendelmeister," it reads. "When it's time for me to die, I don't want to bother anybody. I just want to dig a hole in the back yard, crawl into it, and wait for my consciousness to go away. The problem is I won't be able to cover myself with dirt, and if I die before I get into the hole, well, I won't be able to get into it. Hence I must bother somebody after all. And this, you see, makes dying worth living all the more. Love, F."

CHAPTER M

The copyright data for *The Gay Science: Skygod Edition* indicates that the book will not be published until 2093 by Fostoria University Press, and the purported editor and translator of the edition, Cameron Eliot Vaughn, doesn't appear to exist on any social networks.

Nor does the publisher.

Cameron Eliot Vaughn has likely not yet been born.

Nonetheless, like the translator of the 1974 English edition, Walter Kaufmann, Vaughn begins with a disclaimer about the use of the word "Gay."

Earlier translations used "Joyful," but according to Kaufmann, this word

> quite misses Nietzsche's meaning. *Wissenschaft* means science and never wisdom. He himself called his book: *Die fröhliche Wissenschaft* ('la gaya scienza') [...] Meanwhile, the word "gay" has acquired a new meaning, and people are beginning to assume that it has always suggested homosexuality. But even in the early 1960s that connotation was still quite unusual. (4)

And so on. Today, nobody uses "gay" to denote anything other than sexuality; hence the most recent Penguin Classics edition, translated by R. Kevin Hill, goes by *The Joyous Science.*

One wonders what will happen between now and 2093 to revert the title (for the second time) back to *The Gay Science.* Will gay people finally outnumber straight people? The world would absolutely be a better place, with less wars and more musicals. Nietzsche would approve. Ergo, "gay" in all of its connotations is a perfectly acceptable (and essential) usage. Wake up, Penguin. Open your eyes, ye Little Men of little (in)sight.

CHAPTER N

Gonna pad this chapter with a quote from *The Will to Power*. I do this all the time in my scholarly essays and monographs when I get too lazy to develop my ideas. Sometimes I'll string a bunch of quotes together with bull-shitty syntactic linkages that are written so well they seem like I know what I'm doing. Which I do.

The Will to Power is not one of Nietzsche's formal mono-graphs. It's a selection of notebook entries written between 1883 and 1888 that his sister Elizabeth edited posthu-mously. Some scholars have wrongly grouped it together with the monographs that encompass his canon, most of which include *The Birth of Tragedy* (1872), *Human, All Too Human* (1878), *Daybreak* (1881), *The Gay Science* (1882), *Thus Spoke Zarathustra* (1883), *Beyond Good and Evil* (1886), *On the Genealogy of Morals* (1887), *The Case of Wagner* (1888), *Twilight of the Idols* (1889), and *The Anti-Christ* (1895). *Ecce Homo: How One Becomes What One Is* (1908), then, meta-reflects on this canon like the film *A.I.* meta-reflects on Kubrick's entire filmography. Everything else—*On Truth and Lies in a Nonmoral Sense*, *Philosophy in the Tragic Age of the Greeks*, *Nietzsche contra Wagner*, *Bygone Maestros on the Lunatic Fringe*, *Goethe's Bladder*, etc., etc.—were either unfinished or, like *The Will to Power*, amassed from the *Nachlass* of Nietzsche's wastebasket to capitalize on his fame.

Elizabeth became a Nazi in the twentieth century and was accused of editing her brother's writing with an eye to amplifying latent themes of racism and eugenics. The

Fürher loved it. Thus the Übermensch became an emblem of the Aryan master race.

Here's that quote I promised from *The Will to Power*. It's a good one. It has nothing to do with anything.

"Everything done in weakness fails," writes Nietzsche. "Moral: do nothing" (28).

CHAPTER O

Judge Edmund Durieux can't stop calling people cunt. For example: "Twenty years, ya dirty cunt!" So forth.

This goes on for years.

Eventually the judge receives a formal cease-and-desist letter. The letter says nothing about profanity; vituperation is inherent, subtextual. It reads:

Dear Hoss:

There are bears in the woods. If you go into the woods and stay long enough, you will probably encounter one. Bears are always hungry. I've seen a bear eat a living tree after a full meal of dead elk babies. I have nothing to say about the tree. The elks are another matter. I don't know where the bear got the elks. I imagine it killed and ate their parents, too, but I can't confirm this sad story. The thing is, elks like open fields. They like to run and frolic and live their lives underneath the sky. Bears, on the other hand, prefer the shelter and comfort of darkness. It doesn't make sense that these wild creatures would ever encounter one another. I can't imagine the bear darted out of the woods into a savanna, murdered an elk family, then dragged the children back into the woods to eat them in private. Nor can I imagine an elk family ducking into the woods, even to go to the bathroom. It's all crazy. And yet I saw what I saw. Please bear this in mind, so to speak, as we move forward. I understand that nothing makes sense, but we must do our best to cultivate the garden of nonsense that the Good Lord has installed in our back yard.

Sincerely,
Administration

Judge Durieux knows who wrote the letter: he recognizes a certain secretary's lipstick on the seal. He throws it in the trash unopened. Several days later, a bear roars into the courtroom. Springing onto hind legs, it claws off the bailiff's head, then charges down the aisle, leaps over the bench-rail, and tackles the judge. The jury gasps and shrieks as the animal and the man roll around like lovers on fire. Finally, the bear bites off its victim's head and eats the body. All of the aerial footage occurs in slow motion whereas the death scene and postmortem action unfold in fasttime to an anachronistic background score that doesn't synch with the content.

CHAPTER P

Hello again.

Every administrator in the upper echelon of Fostoria University's Ludovico Campus loves Dio and falls into one of two camps:

1. The ones who prefer "Rainbow in the Dark" to "Holy Diver."

2. The ones who prefer "Holy Diver" to "Rainbow in the Dark."

There is as much in-fighting in this echelon as there is out-fighting among administrators in lesser echelons and among proles in the world at large.

Most sentient human beings prefer "Rainbow in the Dark," but only because of the MTV video that gave it greater exposure in the 1980s. "No 'Holy Diver' video was ever made," Provost Clint McCutchin once proclaimed at a monthly Board of Trustees meeting. "If it had been made, we would be having a different conversation, and the world would be a different place. Alas, we can only work with the tools that Young Goodman Ronnie sees fit to put into our laps and hands."

There was an MTV video for "Holy Diver." The video simply didn't garner as much attention as the one for "Rainbow in the Dark."

This is curious.

"Holy Diver" depicts Ronnie Dio wielding a sword as he sings his way through some kind of alt-Arthurian diegesis, whereas "Rainbow in the Dark" sees him singing lyrics on a city rooftop beneath a cloudy, daytime sky. Pro-Divers have collectively expressed that, given the title "Rainbow in the Dark," one would expect there to at least be a nighttime sky. More to the point: *a rainbow never appears in the video*. Pro-Darks like Provost McCutchin, however, realized that Dio was a canny, self-aware artist and musician who worked in abstractions and knew the value of absence over presence. "'Rainbow in the Dark' is superior precisely because of what it *does not show us*." McCutchin murmurs this thesis in his sleep as often as he communicates it to willing interlocutors.

A lapsed Shakespearean, the Provost has narcolepsy and usually falls asleep during the long, anti-Diver diatribes that made him famous. Alas, look at him now. There he is, leaning against one of Big Boss Hall's ivy-strewn turrets, surrounded by a group of hungover students in their pajamas. They watch him stand and sleep as if they are standing and sleeping themselves. *Beat.* Enter Iago, Richard III, Lady Macbeth, and Claudius, all of whom brandish flaming Molotov cocktails. Apologies: we have slipped into the Provost's psyche. This interstitial, innerspatial diegesis may or may not be authentic. Ay, one thing's for sure: even a court jester can't save us from ourselves … *Exeunt omnes.*

CHAPTER Q

Eggs might be the healthiest things you can eat. They're full of clean fat and protein.

Don't believe naysayers who disparage the yolk and contend that its cholesterol will kill you. It's good cholesterol. And, as with anything you put in your body, moderation is the key.

In this chapter, we will learn how to boil a dozen eggs to perfection. If you don't follow these steps, you're doing it wrong.

Boil water in a big pot on a hot stove. Make sure the water is boiling. Not half-boiling. If the water isn't bubbling like an angry prole, when you put in the eggs, the water will go still for a minute or two. During this period, you will ruin the texture of the egg whites and the consistency of the egg yolks. I don't know why. I just know that these directions are the result of years or trial and error. The Why doesn't matter. Only the Do possesses valence.

Check the eggs to make sure there are no cracks, then submerge them in the boiling water.

If you didn't check for cracks, or if a crack eluded you, the cracked egg(s) will start to leak into the water and dirty it with white curd. This hemorrhage won't taint the batch, but the curd is crummier than you think, and you'll make a mess of things.

Boil the eggs for *exactly 13 minutes*. Any less and the eggs will be underdone. Any more and they will be overdone. Don't fuck up this step.

Remove the pot from the stove and put it in the kitchen sink. Turn on cold water and aim it at the pot. Let the cold water go into the hot water and usurp it. Keep the faucet on for as long as three minutes. Any more than that and you're jogging in place.

Remove the eggs and put them in a dish rack to dry. There's no time limit here. You can actually keep eggs out of the refrigerator for a long while without damaging the innards. Eventually, though, you'll need to put them in the refrigerator and let them go cold.

You can live on eggs as long as you eat a few greens and supplement with healthy carbs (e.g., brown rice and oats), but try not to eat more than nine whole eggs per day. Ten or more is overkill.

CHAPTER R

Judge Durieux makes an example out of everybody that stands before the Man.

If a teenager gets caught shoplifting or drinking wine coolers, for example, he sentences the villain to death. Once he convicted an eight-year-old of looking crossly at his father. "It's in the Bible," he laughed, doing a tap dance on a sound block with a gavel in each hand. He provided no further context for the decision.

There are times when reality has a way of reverting to a watered-down episode of *Game of Thrones* wherein assholes get what they deserve. This happens to Judge Durieux on his seventy-second birthday.

[*Insert revenge scenario here.*]

CHAPTER S

Title for a horror novel about a particularly incompetent university administrator: *The Milquetoast Nightmare.*

CHAPTER T

My first book, *The Kafka Effekt*, a collection of flash fiction and short stories, came out in 2001. Since then, I have published over thirty more book-length works of fiction, nonfiction, theory-fiction, plays, creative nonfiction, literary theory, film criticism, biographies, autobiographies, hagiographies, and now this autohagiography. As one might expect, my readership has grown out of control. It used to be that I could keep up with fan mail, but even now, with a team of personal assistants and show runners opening letters and emails on a daily basis, I rarely have time to read what my readers think of me, and I never have time to respond to their queries.

One of my gentler readers calls himself "Judge Edmund Durieux." He's an older man, and apparently he's been scrutinizing the evolution of my authorship since my first published story, "An Unleashing," which came out in the second issue of an online magazine called *Liquid Fiction* in 1999. I had never received correspondence from Durieux until recently. Stanley Ashenbach, my surrogate personal assistant and literary agent, referred me to an email he sent on Thursday. The subject line read: "What I Enjoy, What I Like, and More." The email itself read:

Dear Dr. Wilson, Mr. Ashenbach, and Other Nonexistent People Affiliated with Wilson's Faux Empire:

Hello! I have always enjoyed dealing with a slightly surrealistic situation and presenting it in a realistic manner. I've always liked fairy tales and myths, magical stories, supernatural stories, ghost stories, surrealistic and allegorical stories. I think they are somehow closer to the sense of reality one feels today than the equally stylized "realistic" story in which a great deal of selectivity and omission has to occur in order to preserve its "realistic" style. In *Lolita*, for example, the character of Quilty is straight out of a nightmare, as are many of the characters in *Dr. Strangelove*. Does this make sense?"

Yours,
Judge Edmund Durieux

Not until the end of the email did I realize that he had bootlegged the entire text from an interview with Stanley Kubrick (Houston 114). I was less concerned with the plagiarized text than I was with my failure to detect the exclusivity of Kubrick's syntax, word usage, and general tone from the very first sentence. I have read that interview many times over for the monograph I'm currently writing on the Kubrickian filmind (a.k.a. the KFM). The interview was conducted in 1971 by Penelope Houston shortly after the release of *A Clockwork Orange*.

I told Stan to write Judge Durieux back and figure out if he had a viable motive for contacting me.

"Be smart," I told Stan, "but play dumb."

Clearly a message had been buried in the email that can only be unburied by learning more about the lawman's backstory, applying his backstory to Kubrick's stolen text, and finally extracting the semiotic venom. Take solace: we're treating the issue like a bottle of wine—we'll get to the bottom of it before lunch …

CHAPTER U

One intoxicated afternoon, Nietzsche's personal assistant Stanley Ashenbach photographed him micturating in a pissoir near a celebrated Leipzig discotheque. Check it out:

See him there having a slash? Nietzsche hated pissoirs and never used them unless he had drank too much.

He preferred sitting on a toilet during the micturation process. That way, nothing would escape the bowl, and he wouldn't have to worry about getting anything on the floor.

"Cleanliness is next to ungodliness," he often joked with interviewers. But he meant it.

Even in public establishments, Nietzsche respected this maxim and acted accordingly. His amoral purity meant as much to him as his personal hygiene and the spaces he inhabited. Everybody knew this.

Hence Stan's photograph caused a stir when it leaked and appeared in every German-speaking tabloid magazine in 1879.

LOCAL PHILOSOPHER BELIES HIS OWN JOKES, read one headline.

At a press conference, Nietzsche explained that the photograph was "the product of a hiccup in my ongoing quest for sobriety."

"I have a lot of regret," he continued. "I am trying to do better. One day, I'm confident that I will become the man who I have always wanted to be."

CHAPTER V

When people cared about the cult of individuality, their actions, accomplishments, and evolutions fed the hungry gullet of their identities, which grew more powerful, more special, more individuated. Culture reveled in the cult. Then everybody became One.

CHAPTER W

I'll always forgive a sonofabitch, but I never forget a fuckin' asshole. You know who you are. If I haven't returned your traumatic favors, rest assured, I will. My vengeance only began with chapter 72.

[*Insert Occam's razor here.*]

CHAPTER X

I don't make a move unless a dream tells me to make one. In the absence of dreams, I doubt that I'd even get a job, let alone raise children and serve as the chief administrator for an Unfamily.

In last night's dream, the Überscreen went blank. I waited for moving pictures to occupy the empty, colorless battlefield. Nothing happened.

Eventually I heard a voice-over say: "My trilogy of biographies on Adolf Hitler, Sigmund Freud, and Frederick Douglass appeared in May 2014, nine years to the month prior to this new volume, which my readers have been asking me to compose since the trilogy's omnibus publication. 'More,' they insisted" (Wilson, *Nietzsche* 19).

Possessed by the demon of a soporific, now-extinct Bronx accent, the voice-over clearly belonged to Stanley Kubrick, who stepped into the diegesis of my unconscious when I was rewatching *The Shining* before bed.

I have watched *The Shining* at least a thousand times. I have taught *The Shining* more times than I can count in my Introduction to Life class. In college, I played Jack Torrence in a stage production of *The Shining* that I wrote and directed. I drink my morning coffee from a *The Shining* mug that features Jack Nicholson's iconic axed-doorway grin. My personalized license plate says THE SHINING, and three years ago, a recovering addict who I met at a sober house taught me to shine. I'm shining you right now. Can you feel it? Can you hear me?

Apparently Kubrick learned to shine as well in 1977 while revising the screenplay. He wasn't prone to method directing, but for a movie of this nature, he told himself, he needed to "get into character." Stephen King knew how to shine, too, and throughout principle photography in 1978 and 1979, the auteur and the author engaged in telekinetic "Shine Wars," remotely hurling chairs, lamps, tables, and other household objects at one another from Kubrick's studio in Hertfordshire, England, and King's home in Lovell, Maine.

As you know, King hated Kubrick's adaptation, claiming that it took advantage of the source material. You also know that the adaptation is far superior to the novel.

CHAPTER Y

Elevator pitch for a big-budget film (based on a novel that I co-write with Donovan Ogg, who will direct):

Ok. Brad Pitt (playing Brad Pitt) time-travels back to the dinosaur era (see *A Sound of Thunder*) just before the Anti-Christ's meteor wipes the fuckers out. Something happens. Pitt goes back and forth a few times and there's a stylish orgy (see *Eyes Wide Shut*). Turns out it's not a meteor; it's aliens (see *2001: A Space Odyssey*), and they live like Morlocks (see *The Time Machine*) inside the Hollow Earth (see *Godzilla vs. Kong*). They come out and kill all the dinosaurs and cover up the genocide for imminent species, making it look like a goddamn meteor. Right? Ok. Pitt befriends a musclebound Phildickian double-agent from off-world (see *Total Recall*), and he finds a way to reverse everything so that the dinosaurs end up killing their would-be murderers instead of the other way around (ha!). Fast-forward to the future. It's, like, bad. The dinosaurs never fucking died, right? Right? Guess what the world looks like now? That's right. It looks like the backyard of my psyche after a pool party fueled by liquor and drugs and whores and gods and demons and philosophers and battles without honor or humanity …

CHAPTER Z

At the end of *Thus Spoke Zarathustra*, the titular narcissist leaves his Cave and rises above the mountains like a morning sun. The day has broken and it belongs to him. Zarathustra has overcome his body, his mind, and his humanity. He shines all day before realizing that nobody sees him—humanity died long ago, and everything is savanna and wind.

Perhaps some more wine, darling …

————•————

APPENDICES

APPENDIX I

Just kidding. I won't bludgeon you with a hammer of appendices. I know you're bored. I won't keep going. Even if I wanted to, my ex-wife wouldn't let me. She always lends me the perspective that enables me to do the right things. This book is over, finally. Say goodbye to *Nietzsche: The Unmanned Autohagiography* once and for all.

APPENDIX II

Maybe one more chapter (viz., "appendix"). Now I kind of want to keep going for awhile.

This is the last biography in the series; I will never do this again—*Nietzsche: The Unmanned Autohagiography* is not just a symptom of the death of the Author, but Death itself. Beyond these words squat an eyeless Abyss. I started getting bored in chapter 4. I guess I needed to get this far to feel good about what I'm doing to you. My ex-wife won't approve of my textual behavior, but she's used to how I renege on my promises. I have reneged on much more than I have articulated here or in *Hitler: The Terminal Biography*, *Freud: The Penultimate Biography*, and *Douglass: The Lost Autobiography*. Read about it after I die in her chronicle of my shortcomings, *Fresh Disappointments: The Complete Saga*. Coming from Fostoria University Press in the not-too-distant future.

APPENDIX III

One more appendix, if you please. A third. In accordance with the screenplay of life, everything happens in threes.

I've exceeded 25k words now. That's about 10k longer than *Hitler: The Terminal Biography*, *Freud: The Penultimate Biography*, or *Douglass: The Lost Autobiography*. I would say I'm running on fumes at this point, but this entire book—the entire biographical tetralogy, in fact—is a product of fumes. Fumes, and fury, and the desire to be nothing less than a man whose accomplishment, like Jean-Jacques Rousseau in his *Confessions* (1782), "will have no imitator. My purpose is to display to my kind a portrait in every way true to nature, and the man I shall portray will be myself" (17).

APPENDIX IV

Go to the next page for the bibliography.

————◆————

BIBLIOGRAPHY

SCHIZE

Abrams, Jerold. "Nietzsche's Overman as Posthuman Star Child in *2001: A Space Odyssey*." *The Philosophy of Stanley Kubrick.* University of Kentucky Press, 2007.

Beerbohm, Max. "All fantasy should have a solid base in reality." *Quotemaster.org.* Web. Accessed December 1, 2022.

Bester, Alfred. "A Diatribe Against Science Fiction." 1961. *Redemolished.* iBooks, 2000.

"D-Girl." Dir. Allen Coulter. S2, E7. *The Sopranos.* HBO, 2000.

"Eastwatch." Dir. Matt Shakman. S7, E5. *Game of Thrones.* HBO, 2017.

Ellison, Ralph. *Invisible Man.* 1952. Vintage, 1980.

Ennui, Donald. "Caught in a Mental State." November 5, 2021. English 2040: Great Books. Fostoria University-Ludovico Campus. Student Essay.

Gibson, William. "Johnny Mnemonic." 1981. *Burning Chrome.* Harper Voyager, 2003.

Jacob, Mary. "Meds, Meltdowns, and Alzheimer's: Frank Sinatra's Manager Tells All on Sad Final Days." *Radar Online.* October 24, 2017. Web. Accessed June 8, 2022.

Job 17.16. *Holy Bible: The Complete Hörnblowér Translation.* Anti-Oedipus Press, 2031.

John 19.5. *Holy Bible: The Complete Hörnblowér Translation.* Anti-Oedipus Press, 2031.

Johnson, Richard. "Frank Sinatra Drank a Bottle of Jack Daily." *Page Six.* December 10, 2014. Web. Accessed June 8, 2022.

Hollingdale, R.J. *Nietzsche: The Man and His Philosophy.* 1965. Oxford University Press, 1999.

Houston, Penelope. "Kubrick Country." 1971. *Stanley Kubrick: Interviews*, ed. Gene D. Phillips. University of Mississippi Press, 2001.

Kaufmann, Walter. "Translator's Introduction." *The Gay Science.* 1882. Vintage, 1974.

Kerr, Imp. "DNA-Based Prediction of Nietzsche's Voice." *The New Inquiry.* March 18, 2015. Web. Accessed May 20, 2022.

Krane, Don Ignatius Falstaff. "Memo to D. Harlan Wilson." December 12, 2021.

Kretz, Robert E. "Book Sucks! It Was Supposed to Be an Autobiography." Review of *Hitler: The Terminal Biography* by D. Harlan Wilson. *Amazon.* October 13, 2017. Web. Accessed May 11, 2022.

Kristeva, Julia. *Powers of Horror.* 1980. In *The Portable Kristeva*, ed. Kelly Oliver. Columbia University Press, 1997.

Lacan, Jacques. *Seminar XX: On Feminine Sexuality—The Limits of Love and Knowledge.* 1975. Trans. Bruce Fink. W.W. Norton & Company, 1999.

McCray, Fay. "Dreams are fragile. Reality is a clumsy postman." *Quotemaster.* Web. Accessed December 1, 2022.

Melville, Herman. *Pierre; or, The Ambiguities.* 1852. Penguin, 1996.

Nabokov, Vladimir. *Invitation to a Beheading.* 1936. Vintage, 1989.

Nietzsche, Friedrich. *Beyond Good and Evil.* 1886. Trans. R.J. Hollingdale. Penguin, 1990.

——. *Ecce Homo*. 1908. Trans. R.J. Hollingdale. Penguin, 2004.

——. *Hairy Gods of the Arcades*. 1951. Anti-Oedipus Press, 2051.

——. *On the Genealogy of Morals*. 1887. Trans. Michael A. Scarpitti. Penguin, 2013.

——. *The Gay Science*. 1882. Trans. Walter Kaufmann. Vintage, 1974.

——. *The Will to Power*. 1901. Trans. R.J. Hollingdale and Walter Kaufmann. Vintage, 1968

——. *Thus Spoke Zarathustra*. 1883. Trans. R.J. Hollingdale. Penguin, 2003.

——. *Twilight of the Idols*. 1889. Trans. R.J. Hollingdale. Penguin, 2003.

No Man's Sky. Version 3.90 for Xbox One. Hello Games, 2016.

Olsen, Lance. *Nietzsche's Kisses*. Fiction Collective 2, 2006.

"Orson Welles Drunk Outtakes for Paul Masson Wine Commercial." *YouTube*. May 26, 2010. Web. Accessed June 2, 2022.

Prideaux, Sue. *I Am Dynamite!: A Life of Nietzsche*. Tim Duggan, 2018.

Reich, James. Review of *Freud: The Penultimate Biography* by D. Harlan Wilson. *The Rumpus*. April 10, 2014. Web. Accessed May 29, 2022.

Rousseau, Jean Jacques. *Confessions*. 1782. Trans. R.S. Pine-Coffin. Penguin, 1953.

Spider-Man. Dir. Sam Raimi. Sony Pictures, 2002.

The Dark Knight. Dir. Christopher Nolan. Warner Brothers, 2008.

The Shining. Dir. Stanley Kubrick. Warner Brothers, 1980.

The World Is Not Enough. Dir. Michael Apted. Metro-Goldwyn-Mayer, 1999.

Thoreau, Henry David. "The Beavers of Yesteryear." 1859. *Selected Essays*. Anti-Oedipus Press, 2016.

Torishima, Dempow. *Sisyphean*. Trans. Daniel Huddleston. Haikosoru, 2013.

Vinivius, Marcus. "Absolutely Not What Is Promised at All." Review of *Freud: The Penultimate Biography* by D. Harlan Wilson. *Amazon*. March 12, 2019. Web. Accessed May 11, 2022.

Wells, H.G. *The Invisible Man*. 1897. Bantam, 2005.

Wells, Jonathan. "Here's How to Drink Like the Rat Pack." *Gentleman's Journal*. n.d. Web. Accessed June 8, 2022.

Whitman, Walt. "Song of Myself." 1855. *Leaves of Grass*. W.W. Norton & Company, 1973.

Wilson, D. Harlan. *Alfred Bester's The Stars My Destination: A Critical Companion*. Palgrave, 2022.

——. "A Peck at My Door." *Exile* 10.3 (Autumn 1998): 7.

——. *Douglass: The Lost Autobiography*. Raw Dog Screaming Press, 2014.

——. *Dr. Identity, or, Farewell to Plaquedemia*. Raw Dog Screaming Press, 2007.

——. *Freud: The Penultimate Biography*. Raw Dog Screaming Press, 2014.

——. *Hitler: The Terminal Biography*. Raw Dog Screaming Press, 2014.

——. *Nietzsche: The Unmanned Autohagiography*. Raw Dog Screaming Press, 2023.

——. *Primordial: An Abstraction*. Anti-Oedipus Press, 2014.

——. *The Kyoto Man*. Raw Dog Screaming Press, 2011.

——. *The Psychotic Dr. Schreber*. Stalking Horse Press, 2019.

——. *Strangelove Country: Science Fiction, Filmosophy, and the Kubrickian Consciousness*. Auteur Publishing, 2024.

Wilson, Harlan. "Re: Lost Autobiography?" Email to D. Harlan Wilson. Nov. 17, 2021.

Woolf, Virginia. *The Waves*. 1931. Penguin, 2019.

Žižek, Slavoj. *Violence*. Picador, 2008.

————— ◆ —————

NIETZSCHE

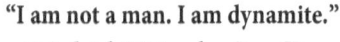

"I am not a man. I am dynamite."
—Friedrich Nietzsche, *Ecce Homo*

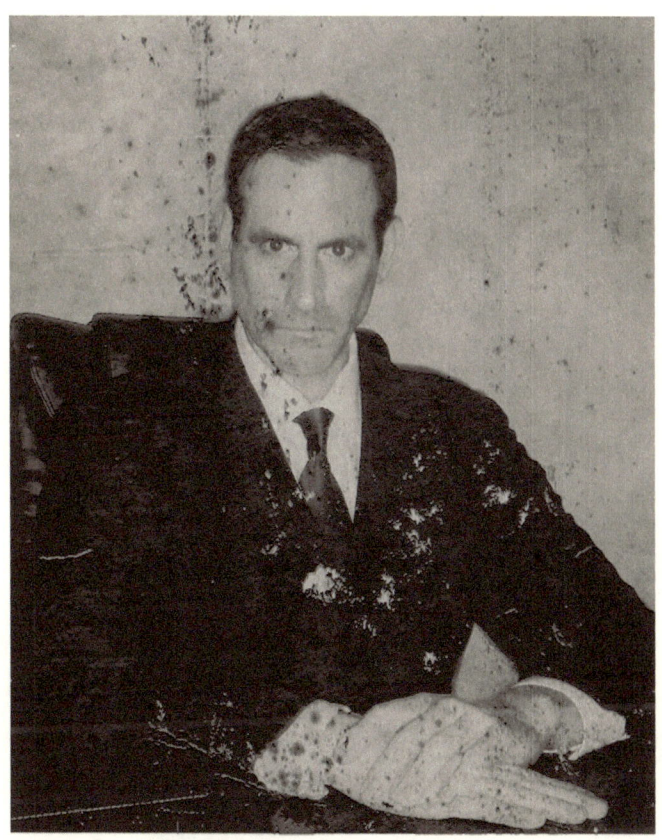

D. HARLAN WILSON was born in Grand Rapids, Michigan, in 1971. He is an American novelist, literary critic, playwright, editor, and college professor, with over 30 book-length works of fiction and nonfiction to his name. He holds two M.A. degrees, one in English from University of Massachusetts-Boston, the other in Science Fiction Studies from University of Liverpool; he received his Ph.D. from Michigan State University in 2005. Hundreds of his stories, essays, and reviews have appeared in magazines, journals, and anthologies across the world in multiple languages. His writing has received nominations for and won numerous awards, among them the Locus Award, the Wonderland Book Award, the Pushcart Prize, the Not the Booker Prize, the Big Other Book Award, the Starcherone Innovative Fiction Prize, and others. Wilson lives in Dreamfield, Ohio, with his daughters Maddie and Renee.

WWW.DHARLANWILSON.COM

DOUGLASS
THE LOST AUTOBIOGRAPHY · D. HARLAN WILSON

WWW.RAWDOGSCREAMING.COM

NIETZSCHE
THE UNMANNED AUTOHAGIOGRAPHY · D. HARLAN WILSON